"You're lucky you didn't marry him, Sunny. He could never have made you happy," Ty Beaumont said.

"How dare you stand there and presume to know what would make me happy?"

"I know, all right. You need a man who'll stand up to you. One who enjoys your spiciness but isn't intimidated by it. One who matches your passion. You need someone who'll make love to you—and often."

"And I suppose you think you fit the bill," Sunny said.

He moved against her then. "You tell me."

"I'll tell you one thing," she said. "I love Don."

"Prove it. Resist me. Resist this."

He backed her against a post supporting the porch roof and branded a fiery kiss on her mouth. Her protests were silenced by his demanding embrace. She tried to turn away, to dodge his persuasive lips, but they held hers relentlessly.

She pushed against his shoulders with the heels of her hands, but he only leaned closer, sandwiching her between him and the smooth cypress wood.

"All this heat," he murmured against her arched neck, "and Jenkins wanted to extinguish it."

"And you don't?"

He brushed his lips back and forth over hers as he shook his head no. "No, Sunny. I want to make you burn hotter. And I want to be in the very heart of your fire. . . ."

WHAT ARE *LOVESWEPT* ROMANCES?

They are stories of true romance and touching emotion. We believe those two very important ingredients are constants in our highly sensual and very believable stories in the *LOVESWEPT* line. Our goal is to give you, the reader, stories of consistently high quality that may sometimes make you laugh, sometimes make you cry, but are always fresh and creative and contain many delightful surprises within their pages.

Most romance fans read an enormous number of books. Those they truly love, they keep. Others may be traded with friends and soon forgotten. We hope that each *LOVESWEPT* romance will be a treasure—a "keeper." We will always try to publish

LOVE STORIES YOU'LL NEVER FORGET
BY AUTHORS YOU'LL ALWAYS REMEMBER

The Editors

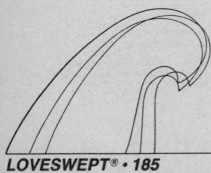

LOVESWEPT® • 185
Sandra Brown
Sunny Chandler's Return

BANTAM BOOKS
TORONTO • NEW YORK • LONDON • SYDNEY • AUCKLAND

SUNNY CHANDLER'S RETURN

A Bantam Book / March 1987

*LOVESWEPT® and the wave device are registered
trademarks of Bantam Books, Inc. Registered in U.S. Patent
and Trademark Office and elsewhere.*

*If you would be interested in receiving protective vinyl
covers for your Loveswept books, please write to this address
for information:*

Loveswept
Bantam Books
P.O. Box 985
Hicksville, NY 11802

ISBN 0-553-21809-3

Published simultaneously in the United States and Canada

*Bantam Books are published by Bantam Books, Inc. Its trade-
mark, consisting of the words "Bantam Books" and the por-
trayal of a rooster, is Registered in U.S. Patent and Trademark
Office and in other countries. Marca Registrada. Bantam
Books, Inc., 666 Fifth Avenue, New York, New York 10103.*

One

"Who is she?"

"Her name is Sunny Chandler."

"You know her?"

"Since third grade."

"Really?"

"Might have been second grade."

"So she grew up here?"

"Yep."

"Where's she been?"

"All your life?"

The first man frowned as he looked down at the second. "Where's she been?" he repeated sternly.

The second man was properly cowed. "New Orleans." His syrupy, Southern accent made the pronunciation "Nawlins." "Moved there a few years back. She's a seamstress."

"A seamstress?" He never would have guessed that by looking at her.

"Something like that. Wanda could tell you more about what she's been doing."

He had every intention of asking the other man's wife later all about this Sunny Chandler. She had aroused his curiosity. And his curiosity, like all his other appetites, never went unappeased for long.

However, for the moment, he was content just to watch Sunny Chandler as she circulated among the other party guests. No longer a small town girl, she stuck out like a sore thumb.

Bad comparison, he thought. Sore thumbs were unsightly. He had yet to find a single unsightly thing about this woman.

"Why did she leave town?" he asked.

His companion chuckled. "You'd never believe it."

"Try me."

"Well, it was like this." In a low voice, the man began to share the juiciest piece of gossip ever to come out of Latham Green.

The subject of the not-to-be-believed tale that was being recounted across the room stifled a bored yawn. The sudden burst of laughter startled her, as it did everyone else nearby. Turning, Sunny saw two men standing by the wall of windows, which overlooked the golf course. The tall blond one was wiping tears of laughter from his eyes.

Probably telling each other dirty jokes, Sunny thought with distaste. These yokels didn't know how to behave in polite company. The back room at the pool hall and this formal parlor of the country club were one and the same to them. They had no sense of decorum.

The bridegroom's family had gone all out for this bash they were hosting in honor of the wedding couple. Since no expense had been spared, the chef had put his best efforts into the buffet. The decorator had depleted the stock of wholesale florists for miles around; the large salon was festooned with bouquets of colorful flowers. While the country club's budget was usually stretched to hire a local sextet for their dances, tonight's music was being provided by a jazzy dance band imported from Memphis.

They weren't bad, either, Sunny thought. She caught the bandleader's roving eye and smiled up at him when they began playing a Kenny Rogers ballad. He winked at her. She winked back, then quickly turned her attention to the buffet. Keeping her head down, she concentrated on filling her plate.

"Sunny Chandler!"

Groaning inwardly, Sunny painted on a fake smile and turned around. "Why, hello, Mrs. Morris."

"Long time no see, girlie."

Eloquent ol' biddy. "Yes, it's been a while."

"How long?"

"Three years." *Three years, two months, six days. Obviously not long enough for people to forget.*

"Are you still in New Orleans?"

"Still there." *And loving it. Loving any place that isn't Latham Green.*

"You're looking good."

"Thank you."

"Very citified."

The observation was intended as a dig. Sunny considered it a supreme compliment. Mrs. Morris crammed a mushroom stuffed with deviled crab into her mouth and chewed vigorously. Then, as though afraid Sunny might run off before she could ply her with more nosy questions, she asked quickly, "And your folks? How are they?"

"Fine, just fine." Sunny turned her back on the woman and picked up a raw oyster on the half-shell—something she wouldn't have eaten in a million years even though she was now a resident of New Orleans—and set it on her plate.

Mrs. Morris, however, wasn't attuned to nuances and had never heard of body language. She went on, undaunted.

"They're still in Jackson?"

"Um-huh."

"They don't come back very often. But then after . . . well, you know what I mean. It's still difficult for them, I'm sure."

Sunny wanted to set down her plate, leave the room, leave the town, leave the parish, just as she had three years ago. The only thing that kept her planted now in front of the melon bowl was the determination not to give anybody the satisfaction of having scared her off.

"Do y'all still own that cabin out on the lake?"

Before Sunny could fashion a response, the honoree of the party came up to her. "Sunny, could I impose on you to help me with my hair? I feel a strategic pin slipping. Please? Excuse us, Mrs. Morris."

Sunny deserted her half-filled plate of food. She hadn't wanted to eat, she'd merely wanted to keep her hands busy. "Thanks," she said beneath her breath as her friend linked arms with her and led her out of the formal salon and down the hall toward the powder room.

Fran was laughing. "You looked as if you needed rescuing. Or maybe Mrs. Morris was the one in peril. I was afraid you were going to eat that Swedish meatball and then skewer her with the toothpick."

They made certain they were alone in the powder room beneath the stairs and locked the door behind them to guarantee privacy. Sunny leaned against the door and drew an exasperated breath. "And you wonder why this is my first time back in three years. Do you blame me for staying away? She was all but frothing at the mouth, crazed with a lust to know all the titillating details of my life in the big city."

Fran was sitting at the aproned vanity table repairing her lipstick. "Are there any titillating details of your life in the big city?" She cast Sunny a teasing glance in the oval, framed mirror. Sunny's icy stare only evoked another laugh.

"Relax, Sunny. This is Small Town, U.S.A. What else have people like Mrs. Morris got to do?"

"Watch the grass grow?"

"Right. They have to occupy themselves with each other's business. And, let's be frank, you gave them a lot of material to work with several years ago."

"I wasn't trying to get their attention."

"Well, you got it anyway. For all these years, they've been dying to know why you did what you did. Your parents moved away soon afterward, so they were no help in supplying an answer to the riddle. Now you show up looking like a character straight off the set of *Dynasty*, by all appearances unscathed by the incident. They're dying to know what prompted you to do such an unheard-of thing. Can you blame them for being curious?"

"Yes, I can blame them. The gossips practically drove my parents nuts with their childish curiosity. Mom and Dad couldn't go anywhere without being on the receiving end of snide looks and prying questions. Even so-called friends pestered them about it. They bowed to the pressure and left."

"I thought they left because your dad got that job in Jackson."

"That's the reason they gave me, but I never believed it. *I* was the reason they relocated. I've got to live with that, Fran." She took a lipstick from her miniclutch and dabbed her lips with it.

"But thanks for the compliment about me looking like one of the women in *Dynasty*."

Fran smiled. "Ladies around here wear either short cocktail dresses or long formals. They never heard of matinee length. All their hems are even, not raggedy like yours. No one would think of putting tangerine and violet together, but it looks sensational on you," she said, admiring Sunny's dress. It looked like the artful crisscrossing and draping of several scarves.

"And, my word, my word," Fran exclaimed, clapping her cheeks in theatrical horror, "have you really got *two* holes pierced in one ear? You're bound to be a pinko! I wouldn't be at all surprised if there were a Yankee or two in your family tree."

Laughing, Sunny swatted the air inches from Fran's nose. "Be quiet! You're making me laugh, and I don't want to laugh."

Fran clasped Sunny's hand warmly. "I know you didn't want to come back here, and that the only reason you did was for my wedding. I realize what a sacrifice it was, and I appreciate it."

"I wouldn't have missed your wedding, Frannie. You know that. Although . . ."

"Although you don't understand why I want to get married again," Fran finished for her.

"Something like that."

Sunny stared earnestly into Fran's eyes. It seemed to her that Fran was only digging a deeper rut for herself. She had had a chance to take her two children and leave this backwater town after obtaining a divorce from her first husband. But Fran had stayed, stuck out all the gossip, and was getting married again.

"Sunny, I love Steve. I want to marry him, have a baby with him." Fran's expression pleaded for understanding. "I thought I was in love with Ernie, but I only saw what everybody else did, a dashing football hero. Unfortunately, that was the sum total of what he was. When he couldn't be that anymore, he fell apart, turned to drinking, turned to other women. They still cheered him on instead of telling him to grow up as I, the nagging wife, did.

"Well, Steve's as solid as the Rock of Gibraltar. He loves me, he loves the girls. He's not as handsome as Ernie, and he hasn't got that built-like-a-brick-outhouse body, but he's a real man, not an overgrown child."

Sunny patted Fran's hand. "I'm happy for you. You know that. I think the world of Steve for making you whole again. It's just that I can't imagine anybody actually choosing that kind of life. I feel lucky to have escaped it."

"Only because you haven't found the right man to share it with." Fran arched her brow. "Speaking of which, I don't suppose you've seen your ex-fiancé."

"No, and I hope I don't." Sunny fiddled with her hair. "He and Gretchen are still married, I suppose."

"Yes, but one hears things. The scuttlebutt is that—"

"No!" Sunny said. "I don't want to know. I won't stoop to the level of everybody else in town and yearn for the latest gossip." She looked at Fran's hairdo critically. "Your hair is perfect. Where's that slipping pin you mentioned?"

"That was only a ploy to get you away from Mrs. Morris." Fran popped up off the vanity stool in a movement almost too spry for a thirty-year-old mother of two children.

The friends left the powder room, giggling like girls, the way they had done through junior and senior high school. Fran drew a more serene face when they reentered the salon. Her intended spotted her and moved toward her and Sunny.

"Hon, the president of the company just arrived from Baton Rouge," Steve told her. "He can't wait to meet you. Says he wants to see the woman who convinced a confirmed old bachelor like me to get married. 'Xcuse us, Sunny."

"Surely."

She watched as the successful insurance executive whisked his future bride away to meet his boss. Steve proudly introduced Fran and her two young daughters. Sunny was delighted over Fran's newfound happiness. After being married to Ernie, she certainly did deserve it.

Steve placed a protective and proprietary arm around Fran's slender shoulders. Sunny saw the instinctive, unconscious gesture. It wordlessly conveyed the way Steve felt about his future wife. Sunny attributed the empty feeling that suddenly seized her to hunger and decided to give the buffet another try.

As if returning to Latham Green hadn't been bad enough in itself, it was adding insult to injury that she had had to return for a wedding. Don, the man she had almost married, was a subject she knew she would be faced with. At least she had survived the first mention of his name and didn't have to dread that milestone any longer.

Talking about him had brought back all the negative emotions she had left behind her three years ago. She had thought she was rid of them for good, but it seemed that they had been perching like gremlins on the city limit signs, just waiting for her to return. The moment she had, they had reclaimed her.

She should have known better than to come back. But how could she refuse Fran's request to attend her second wedding? She couldn't. Nor would Fran settle for her appearing only at the ceremony and making a hasty getaway afterward. Before she realized what had happened, Sunny had committed herself to attending this party and staying until after the wedding. While she was here she planned to take care of some business, but she still had to live through the week. One week. One week in a town she had sworn never to see again. Would she survive it?

Perhaps. But not without compensations. Compensations like indulging a craving or two, she thought as she eyed the array of desserts at the end of the buffet table. Little transgressions like that would help to keep her sane. She deserved a reward, didn't she? How could she lend Fran moral support if she didn't fortify herself with little treats?

Before she could talk herself out of it, she took two triple-chocolate-dipped strawberries from a silver tray and found a secluded corner in which to eat them. Forbidden fruit they were, if a woman wanted to maintain a svelte figure. But forbidden fruit was just the kind Sunny needed at the moment.

Holding the tiny green stem between her thumb and finger, she bit into the first strawberry. The dark chocolate outer layer was bittersweet against her tongue. Then the milk chocolate coated the roof of her mouth with its rich, velvet texture. Next, almost like a benediction, the mellow white chocolate soothed her palate and prepared it for the succulent, ruby fruit her teeth sank into.

She chewed it with slow, sinful relish, letting each layer of chocolate melt and fill her mouth with its particular degree of sweetness.

It was a sensuous experience, not only for Sunny, but for the man watching her from across the room. Casually propped against the wall, ankles crossed, long legs at a slant, he watched Sunny Chandler's carnal destruction of two chocolate-covered strawberries. She made eating them such an erotic exercise that his own mouth watered, more for a taste of the lips and tongue that did them such delectable justice than for the strawberries themselves.

"Still got your eye on her, I see."

He shifted his weight, but didn't remove his gaze from the woman. "Sunny Chandler's an eyeful," he admitted to the man who had rejoined him.

"Always was. One of the prettiest girls in school. Classy, you know?"

"What she did before she left wasn't very classy. Why'd she do it?"

"Well now, if I knew that, I'd be the only one."

The taller man looked down at his friend. "Oh, yeah? She just pulled a stunt like that and left?"

"Like that." He snapped his fingers. "Left her bridegroom—Don Jenkins, you know him—high and dry." He jabbed the other man in the ribs. "No pun intended."

They laughed together, but not loud enough to detract attention from the future bride and groom, who were busy opening wedding gifts amid appreciative *oohs* and *aahs*.

"She was supposed to marry Don Jenkins, huh?"

"Yeah. I never go into the Baptist church that I don't think about it."

"And nobody knew why she walked out?"

"Uh-uh. 'Course, there was plenty of speculation."

All it took was an inquiring, arching eyebrow and the second man was only too glad to fill the first in on a few of the possibilities that had been discussed over card tables and clotheslines.

He pondered the woman a moment longer and watched as she stopped a passing waiter to hand him her plate. "I think I'll ask the lady to dance."

He pushed his upper body away from the wall,

but the other man's laughter halted him. "Good luck, buddy."

"You sound as though you think I'll need it."

"You couldn't touch her with a ten-foot pole."

"I don't want to touch her with a ten-foot pole. I want to take her to bed."

The other man started with surprise. He'd never heard his friend say anything so bold. Oh, he would talk man talk, all right, swap bawdy stories. But his tales were always about somebody else. He kept his private life to himself. He didn't have to toot his own horn. His success rate was well known around town.

He recovered from his surprise. "I know that your track record with women is impressive. But it ain't gonna happen this time."

"What makes you think so?"

"From what I hear, Sunny is a real balls-breaker. She doesn't have anything whatsoever to do with men. Turns 'em to stone like that gal in Greek mythology."

Rather than deterring the man, that piece of information only served to pique his curiosity more. He always welcomed a challenge. His eyes narrowed as he continued to stare at her.

His cohort recognized that speculative look. "I know what you're thinking. But you can't thaw that one out."

"Are you losing confidence in me?"

"Where Sunny Chandler is concerned I am."

The sly grin was slow in coming. "What do you want to bet?"

"You mean it?" He got an affirmative nod. The man absently tugged on his earlobe as he contemplated the wager. "I had a hankering for a new fly-casting rod, but Wanda cracked a crown and had to get a new one. What dentists charge for those things these days—"

"A new fly-casting rod it is. And you know how I like Wild Turkey. Shall we say a case of Wild Turkey against a new fly-casting rod?"

They shook hands solemnly. "She'll hightail it back to New Orleans as soon as this wedding is over. You don't have much time. One week from tonight."

"I don't need much time." He moved away.

"Wait," the other man said, detaining him a second time. "How'll I know if you pull it off?"

"By the smile on her face."

His smile had all the cunning of a fox and all the honesty of a Boy Scout. Piratical mischief and angelic sincerity exuded from that smile. That self-confident grin could either make you melt or shiver, depending upon your point of view. Sunny did a little of both when she met it seconds later.

At the tap on her shoulder, she turned around, confronting a red necktie with thin blue stripes resting against a dove-gray shirt. She followed the necktie up to that devastating smile.

Her heart skipped a beat or two. Her stomach seemed to free-fall for a long time before crash landing. Her mouth went as dry as the Sahara. But she kept her features cool and remote as she took in the streaked blond hair, Nordic blue eyes, a suntanned face, and tall, muscular frame. She recognized him as the man who had laughed out loud so rudely.

His packaging was prettier than most. So? She knew the type. She recognized that kind of smile. He was all but licking his chops, thinking that he'd spotted a tasty morsel. Well, he'd find out soon enough that she was more vinegar than honey.

"I like the way you eat strawberries."

That wasn't exactly the opening line Sunny had expected. At least she gave him credit for original-

ity. Cerebrally she could acknowledge his clever-
ness and pass it off. Physically it wasn't so easy to
dismiss.

Her tummy fluttered and slipped a little lower.
That leading line of so few words told her several
things at once. That he'd been watching her for
some time. That he liked what he saw. That he
was interested enough to take a closer look.

Flattering? Yes. Had she been any other woman,
it might have worked for him. Instead she only
stared back at him with a hauteur that would
have discouraged a less determined man.

His sapphire gaze moved down to her mouth.
"What else are you good at?"

"Fending off unwelcomed passes."

He laughed. "And making witty comebacks."

"Thank you."

"Dance?"

"No thank you."

She tried to turn her back on him, but he
touched her elbow. "Please?"

"No. Thank you." She enunciated the words so
that he couldn't mistake the resolve behind them.

"How come?"

She didn't want to embarrass Fran and Steve.
Otherwise she would have reminded this glib, blue-
eyed blond man with the to-die-for body and the
crocodile grin that she owed him absolutely no
explanation for not wanting to dance with him.

Instead she settled for, "I've danced too much
already and my feet are hurting. Now, excuse me,
please."

She moved away, keeping her back to him. She
stepped around the buffet and headed toward the
round table in the center of the room, the one
with the champagne fountain on it. She held a
tulip glass under one of the spouts and filled
it.

"I was taught in Sunday school that it's a sin to lie."

Champagne splashed over her hand as she spun around, making eye contact with that broad chest again. She seriously doubted that he'd ever been to Sunday school. And she was positive that the only thought he ever gave to sin was which one to commit next. "*I* was taught that it's rude to make a pest of oneself."

"You didn't have to lie, you know."

"I wasn't lying."

He made a *tsk*ing sound. "Now, Miss Chandler, I've been watching you for more than an hour, and you haven't danced a single dance, though you've been invited to several times."

Her cheeks went pink, but she was more annoyed than embarrassed. "Then that should have been your first clue. I don't want to dance."

"Why not just say so?"

"I just did."

He laughed again. "I like your sense of humor."

"I wasn't trying to be amusing and couldn't care less whether you like me, my sense of humor, the way I eat strawberries, or anything else."

"You've made that clear enough, but, you see, that creates a bit of a problem for us."

"How?" She was quickly losing patience and tiring of his game. If it hadn't been for Mrs. Morris's avaricious stare, she would have set down her champagne glass and stalked from the room, making her apologies to Fran and Steve later. "What problem could you and I possibly have in common?"

"See that man standing over there by that basket of roses?"

"Who? George Henderson?"

"You remember him?"

"Of course." Sunny smiled and waved. Blushing

to the roots of his thinning hair, George waved back.

"Well," the stranger continued, "George and I just made a wager."

"Oh?"

"He bet a new fly-casting rod against a case of Wild Turkey that I couldn't get you into bed with me by the end of next week. Now, unless you care just a little bit whether I like you or not, it's going to be damned hard for me to win my case of whiskey."

He carefully removed the tilting champagne glass from her bloodless, nerveless fingers before it spilled. Setting it on the table first, he then pulled her into his arms and said, "Dance?"

The band was into the second verse of the song before Sunny could speak. "You are kidding, aren't you?"

Butter would have melted beneath his smile. "Now what do you think?"

She didn't know what to think. She didn't know a man with enough guts to admit making such a wager, if he'd had enough gall to make that kind of bet in the first place. Surely he was teasing her! Still, his smile wasn't very reassuring.

She didn't smile back. "What do I think? I think you don't take no for an answer."

"Not when I want something badly enough."

"And you badly wanted to dance with me?"

"Uh-huh."

"Why?"

"I've never met a woman with golden eyes before."

Those very eyes blinked up at him. "They're not gold. They're light brown."

"I'd call them golden," he replied stubbornly. "They match your name. Wonder how your mother knew ahead of time to name you Sunny?"

She quickly realized that George Henderson

would have told him her name. No need for alarm there. But he couldn't have determined the color of her eyes from across the room, and she pointed out that discrepancy to him. "So why did you want to dance with me?"

He drew her closer. "As I said, I like the way you eat chocolate-covered strawberries." Eyes the color of a Scandinavian fjord looked down at her mouth again. "There's a tiny speck of chocolate in the left corner of your lips." Instinctively, Sunny made a point of the end of her tongue and searched out the particle. When it dissolved against her tongue, he said, "Got it."

Sunny jerked herself out of the momentary trance he had miraculously induced. "I guess George told you everything about me."

"Enough. But some things I want to find out for myself."

"Like what?"

"What I want to know about you, Sunny, I don't think you'd want me to find out here on the dance floor."

She squirmed away from him and said frostily, "Thank you for the dance, Mr.—"

"Beaumont. Ty Beaumont. But you can't stop dancing now. They're already into another song." He swung her into his arms again. When she would have struggled to extricate herself, he said, "Hi, Fran. Hi, Steve. Great party."

"Hello, Ty," they said in unison.

Sunny gave them a sickly smile as they danced past, then shot her partner a poisonous glance. He had her and he knew it. He wasn't going to let her go without a fuss, and he knew that she wouldn't risk making a scene.

But she'd be damned before she relaxed her body against his, the way his strong arms were dictating that she should. It was disconcerting enough just to be held this close. His thighs were hard as they moved against hers.

"Back to why I wanted to dance with you," Ty said conversationally. "I like your golden hair, too."

"Thank you."

"Bet it looks sexy as hell spread out on a pillow."

"You'll never know."

"I've already got one bet riding on that. Wanna make one between you and me?"

"No."

"Good. Because you'd lose."

"On the contrary, it would be a sure win, Mr. Beaumont. And please remove your hand."

"From here?" He pressed the small of her back. There was an explosion of heat in Sunny's lower body. She almost gasped at the shock of it, but caught herself just in time. She was afraid, however, that she hadn't concealed her reaction from her partner, who was watching her closely. "Relax," he told her.

"Forget it."

"I don't mean to be insulting."

"Don't you?"

"No. I just admire your figure."

"Well, if you must, please admire it from afar."

"I'd be the first one to jump to your defense if any other man held you this close. But since we're going to be intimate, I—"

"We are *not* going to be intimate."

He smiled knowingly.

Sunny's stiff smile was strictly for the benefit of all the Mrs. Morrises crowding the room. She was not only annoyed but afraid. Ty Beaumont transmitted a masculine, animalistic vitality that beckoned to every female of the species. Sunny, for all her imperviousness where men were concerned, was still a female. Apparently she wasn't as immune to pure sexual magnetism as she had thought. To keep herself from responding to it, it was mandatory to direct the conversation into safer channels.

"When did you move to Latham Green, Mr. Beaumont?"

"Make it Ty. Let's see," he said, wrinkling his forehead in concentration, "about three years ago. Guess we just missed each other."

Sunny reasoned that George had told him when she had moved away. Before she could ask if George had told him the circumstances of her leaving he said, "In a room full of polyester, your silk really stands out."

He rubbed his hand over her back. Reflexively she arched it. A wrong move. Because it caused her breasts to flatten against the solidity of his chest. The blue eyes grew dark and intense. Sunny sucked in her breath sharply.

"What do you do for a living?" she asked thinly.

"I'll bet you wear silk undies, too."

Suddenly Ty was holding nothing but air. Sunny was moving away from him, making quiet, unobtrusive apologies to the people she edged around on her way to the door. Because of his size, it was more difficult for Ty to cut and wend his way through the dancing couples. Sunny had reached the front steps of the country club's colonial facade before he caught up with her.

"Was it something I said?"

She faced him like a spitting cat. "It was everything you said, everything you did. I despise that stupid, masculine superiority that you emanate like a bad odor. In fact I wholly dislike every sexist thing about you, Mr. Beaumont. Now, leave me alone."

"All right, look, I'm sorry, maybe I was coming on a little too strong."

"A little too strong?"

"I saw you and I wanted to take you to bed. So—"

He was talking to her back again. He jogged down the steps to the gravel drive that was doing serious damage to Sunny's pastel leather heels. He caught her arm; she wrested it free.

"If you get your kicks from talking dirty, Mr. Beaumont, I suggest you go to Bourbon Street. There are girls there you can pay by the minute to listen to that garbage. But please spare me from listening to it."

"George gave me the impression that you're not like the women around here."

"Thank heaven for that."

"You lead a singles life in the city."

"Right."

"So I was just going straight to the heart of the matter. We've only got a week."

"Of course. Why waste time?" she said, dripping sarcasm from every syllable.

"A sophisticated woman like you knows the score. I saw you, wanted you, I made my move. If I read you wrong, you have my sincerest apology. I wouldn't want to offend you."

"I can't tell you how much I appreciate that."

"So, do we plan a roll in the sack for later in the week or not?"

She stared at him, momentarily speechless. But he looked like he actually expected an answer. Finally she said, "No, Mr. Beaumont, we do not."

He grinned disarmingly. "Sure?"

She crossed her arms over her middle and assumed the aggravated stance and expression that had burst innumerable masculine egos. "Not unless hell freezes over, Mr. Beaumont."

He wasn't the least put off. Indeed, he moved closer, so close that she had to tilt her head back to look up at him. "Then you don't play fair. You should have just come right out and told me that, Sunny," he said in a throbbing voice, "instead of getting all warm and fluid while we were dancing."

Sunny stared up at him with mortification, not only because his words were so provocative, but because they were so accurate. "I . . . you . . . I didn't get warm an . . . an . . . and fluid."

He peered at her from beneath a shelf of unruly dark blond brows. "You've already got one lie to your credit, Sunny. I wouldn't go pushing my luck if I were you."

"I'm not lying!"

His eyes slid down her middle. "Want me to prove it?"

She spun on her heels, which wasn't too easy to do in the loose gravel, and stormed toward her car. Ty, grinning from ear to ear, watched her get into an American sports car and drive away as though the devil were after her. In essence that was exactly who was after her, Ty thought with a lecherous grin.

"I warned you you'd strike out," George said, joining him under the porte cochere.

"This is just the first inning, George. Don't start making space above the mantel for all the fishing trophies you're going to catch with that new rod," Ty said confidently. "A lot can happen in a week."

George seemed equally as confident of Ty's failure. "A week isn't much time."

In her car, Sunny was speeding down the highway. "A week!" she exclaimed. It would seem like an eternity.

Two

She had forgotten how hot the sun could be out on the lake. Fran and she had spent hours lying on beach towels spread out on this very pier, basted in suntan oil so thick they could trace the initials of their latest beaux on their thighs, bellies, chests.

How they had giggled! How catty they'd been, speculating if this girl really *did*, as everyone said she did, wondering if this boy was as good a kisser as his smug girlfriend claimed, weighing Warren Beatty's merits against those of Paul Newman.

Everything had been such fun then. Growing up in a small town hadn't been so disagreeable. Maybe that was the problem; she had simply outgrown the town. She was no longer a small town girl. Now she belonged in the city.

New Orleans was a laid back city in comparison with many others, but even at that, it couldn't offer this sublime serenity. She'd forgotten how quiet the country could be. The hustle and bustle and clamorous noise of the city seemed far away. For at least today, she had nothing to do but lie here in the sun and soak up the silence and the glorious heat.

For most people the heavy, humid heat would be stifling. Sunny loved it. She welcomed its blanketing embrace. The sun's rays seeped into her skin like mystical healing powers, inducing a delicious torpor, a state of utter laziness.

There was very little breeze, but occasionally a breath of it would stir the tops of the cypress trees lining the shore. On the horizon enormous white thunderclouds were building up. They were empty threats of evening showers that rarely materialized. The lake was still, its surface glassy. Sunny liked the sound of the water lapping at the piling beneath the dock. Insects droned around her. Dragonflies skimmed the surface of the lake, sometimes rippling the water with their fragile, sheer wings.

Their buzzing sound, combined with the rhythmic, slapping sound of water against the piling, was hypnotic. She dozed.

"You've got a lot of nerve."

Sunny sat up, grabbing the top of her bikini in the process. Her heart was in her throat. Bright yellow dots exploded against a field of black in front of her eyes. She had sat up too fast and didn't immediately regain her vision or her equilibrium. When she did, she muttered a curse.

Ty Beaumont was hauling himself onto her dock and securing his small fishing boat to one of the piles.

"You're the one with a lot of nerve, Mr. Beaumont. You scared me half to death!"

"Sorry." His grin said otherwise. "Were you asleep?"

"I must have dozed off."

"Didn't you hear my motor?"

"I thought it was a bug."

"A bug?"

"A dragonfly."

He looked at her warily. "How long have you been out in this sun?"

"Forget it," Sunny said, and uttered a long-suffering sigh.

She couldn't lie back down. It was bad enough having to look up at him from a sitting position. She stubbornly refused to secure the neck strap of her bikini. The bra was snug and stretchy enough to stay up by itself. She wasn't about to give him the satisfaction of seeing her rattled. Groping for and tying the straps would make her look like a flustered old maid in the company of her first gentleman caller. Well, she wasn't an old maid. And he sure as hell wasn't a gentleman.

He plopped down on the bare deck beside her. "Won't you have a seat?" she asked sweetly.

He merely grinned again. "Thanks."

To give herself something to do besides stare into his mirrored sunglasses and wonder what part of her exposed body he was looking at, she took off her own sunglasses and unnecessarily cleaned the tinted lenses with a corner of her towel. "What are you doing here?"

"I was fishing on the lake and just happened to see you sprawled out here, lying half naked. That's why I said you've got a lot of nerve. You were issuing an open invitation to any pervert on the lake to come over here and take a gander, possibly do you bodily harm."

"I've been sunbathing on this pier practically all my life, and no one has ever bothered me before. In fact, you can't even see this dock from the open lake. You have to come into the cove. And as far as I know, there's never been a pervert on Latham Lake . . . until now."

His laughter was deep and richly masculine.

"Well, I've admitted to being interested in your body, but I wouldn't do anything too perverted." He paused for several beats. "Unless you like it that way."

Sunny got the impression that he winked behind his sunglasses. She hastily began tossing things into her canvas beach bag. Paperback book. Sun visor. Transistor radio. Deciding to leave her towel where it was for the present, she stood up and began stalking barefoot across the planks.

"Where're you going?"

His arm shot out. Sunny gasped. His hard fingers encircled one of her ankles. He didn't make her stumble, but he effectively stopped her in her tracks just the same.

"Indoors. I prefer sunbathing in private. Beyond that, I don't want to swap sexual innuendos with you, Mr. Beaumont."

"Chicken?"

"No!"

"Then come back."

It was a challenge Sunny had to accept. But she would have agreed to anything just to get his strong fingers from around her ankle. The contact was shooting alarming sensations up her leg and into her thigh. She worked her ankle from his firm grip and sat back down on the towel, her expression mutinous.

"I was only being neighborly." She glanced at him with patent disbelief. "I was," he said defensively. "I was only trying to make you feel welcome."

"I don't need the welcome mat rolled out. I grew up here, remember?"

"Then by comparison that makes me the newcomer. You should be nice to me."

She trapped a smile just before it broke across her lips. Give this man an inch and he'd take endless miles. He needed no encouragement, not even a simple smile. Sunny only wished his charm was easier to ward off.

He was dressed in cutoffs and a faded, sleeveless shirt, which was opened almost to his waist. She couldn't help but notice that his chest was muscled and matted with crinkly, sweat-curly, dark blond hair. He had nice legs, too, if you liked hard, well-shaped muscles, tanned skin, and sungilded body hair. He wasn't wearing any socks with his tennis shoes. And he had on a bill cap.

Sunny associated bill caps with baseball players and rednecks with "Honk if you're horny" bumper stickers on their muddy pickup trucks. Neither type appealed to her. But Ty Beaumont under a bill cap wasn't bad at all. Perhaps because of his blond hair curling around the sides of it, and the way he wore it low on his brow right above his opaque sunglasses. When he smiled, his teeth shone whitely in his bronzed face.

His shirt clung damply. There were beads of perspiration trickling down his neck and making sodden points out of strands of his hair. Sunny rarely saw a man sweating. The men she came into contact with were usually inside air-conditioned buildings. They were dressed in business suits and ties. They always had on socks.

Beaumont was a shock to her system, that was all. The scent of sweat and sunshine and lake water on a man was new to her.

That was the only way she could account for her accelerated pulse and the fact that the bottom had fallen out of her stomach. She wanted to run just as fast as she could back into the security of her cabin. But she couldn't retreat without losing face. So, she would stay and be "nice" to him if it killed her.

"Catch anything?" she asked, nodding down toward the boat.

He leaned back, stretching his long legs out and propping himself up on one elbow. "Not yet."

His simple answer vibrated with undertones that made Sunny uncomfortably aware of just how skimpy her bikini was. It was the color of cayenne and set off her golden coloring to full advantage. She wished she had brought along the jungle print sarong that went with it. A cover-up hadn't seemed necessary when she left the cabin. Now she longed for one. A T-shirt, a robe, a bear rug, anything to shield her from Ty Beaumont's gaze. She couldn't see it behind his glasses, but she could *feel* it moving over her, resting on places that felt abnormally warm.

"It's hot today," she said briskly.

"And getting hotter."

"Almost too hot to fish." Her eyes narrowed suspiciously. Her father was a fisherman. In the summertime he went out early in the morning, while it was still relatively cool and the lake was shrouded with mist. He never went out in his fishing boat in the heat of the day. An accusation was forming in her mind, but he spoke before she had a chance to.

"I bet you love the heat."

"I do," Sunny admitted. "How did you know?"

"You're a very sensuous woman."

"What makes you say that?"

"Lots of things. I watched you yesterday at the party."

He crossed his legs more comfortably. At least the readjustment made *him* more comfortable. It unnerved Sunny considerably. She swallowed hard as she glanced down at the impressive bulge between his thighs. The aged denim cutoffs had conformed to the shape of his body years ago. They kept no secrets.

"I noticed your ankle bracelet right away." He

reached out and, with his index finger, followed the slender gold chain around her ankle. "There's not another woman in Latham Green who wears an ankle bracelet."

"Have you personally verified that statistic?"

"An educated guess," he said, taking no offense at her mild rebuke. "It's not a piece of jewelry that the majority of women wear. Only women with intensely passionate natures."

She jerked her foot away from his hand. "That's crazy." Sunny wished that her voice had more impetus behind it and didn't sound so breathy. "I bought it because I like it. I think it's pretty."

"You bought it for yourself?"

"What's wrong with that?"

"A man didn't give it to you?"

"No."

"That's a damn shame."

"Why?"

"Installing it would have made for one helluva private party." He grinned broadly.

"Look, Mr. Beaumont, I don't know what my *former* friend George told you about me—"

"Oh, he told me plenty, but I formed my own opinions."

"In the ten minutes that we were together?"

"Before we even met," he said easily. "Did you realize that you mouthed the words to every song the band played last night?"

Sunny was about to argue when she decided that denying it was pointless. Singing along with the radio was a habit of hers. "I like music."

"And food. I've already told you that your mouth does more for a strawberry than shortcake and whipped cream."

"You make eating a strawberry sound lewd."

"It bordered on it," he said softly.

Sunny had no effective comeback prepared and

decided that if such were the case, it would be more prudent to say nothing. Even when she was at her most acerbic, he seemed to be ready with a glib rejoinder.

"You selected food from the buffet very carefully. Food with eye appeal. Everything you put on your plate was . . . pretty." He smiled as though "pretty" was a word he didn't use frequently. "Except for the oyster, of course, and you only took that because Mrs. Morris was annoying you."

Sunny's mouth formed a small o. Just how long *had* he watched her? But more startling than the time involved was his accurate perception of her. She felt exposed and vulnerable. "You should have become a window peeper."

"How do you know I'm not?" At her stunned expression, he laughed. "Relax. I'm not that subtle. Nor that masochistic. If I'm interested in a woman, I want to do more than peep at her from the bushes. I want to touch."

He picked up her plastic bottle of suntan oil and poured a drop into his palm. He sniffed it. "Smells like a drink from Trader Vic's bar."

"That's why I bought it."

"I'm not surprised. Several times last night I saw you smelling the flowers."

He was rubbing the oil between his palms. The slow, rotating motion of his large hands was getting to Sunny. She blinked rapidly to stave off the trance she felt stealing over her like a fog. "I like perfume." She noticed suddenly that she was very thirsty. Her tongue was sticking to the roof of her mouth. "I love anything perfumed. Flowers, suntan oil, anything."

"Have you ever been into that perfumery in New Orleans?"

"The one on Royal?"

"I forget exactly. Somewhere in the French Quarter." He was rubbing his thumbs along the tips of his fingers, coating them with the slick oil. "I spent an entertaining hour in there once, selecting perfume."

"For whom?" She'd been watching the movement of his fingers too long. Their wanton enjoyment of the suntan oil had made her drowsy. The question popped out before she realized she'd spoken it. When she did, she snapped back to attention.

"My mother."

"I should have guessed."

His smile was lazy. "I didn't realize until then that fragrance is a science."

"The formulas are carefully guarded."

"I don't mean how it's made." He sat up straight and leaned close. "I was talking about the science of applying it."

Sunny wished he would take off his glasses. It was disconcerting to talk to her own image in their mirrored lenses. But now, when he granted her unspoken wish and removed them, she wanted him to replace them immediately. His eyes were much more unsettling than the opaque sunglasses.

"I always thought it was correct for a woman to dab perfume behind her ears and on her wrists."

"It is," Sunny said gruffly.

"Yes, but it evaporates more quickly there. Perfume should either be applied with cotton or sprayed on. I didn't know until I visited the shop that putting it on with a finger taints what is left in the bottle."

"It has something to do with one's own body acid, I believe."

"And this lady explained to me that to get the maximum benefit of any fragrance, where it blends with a woman's body heat and emanates the scent every time she moves, she should apply it to—"

"I've really got to go in."

"—her hair . . . her breasts . . . her stomach . . . her . . . thighs."

His eyes touched each spot as he spoke the particular word. On the last word, his eyes stayed in the vicinity of Sunny's lap. "Tell me, Sunny, being the sensuous woman you are, have you ever applied perfume to your"—his gaze moved up with agonizing slowness—"hair?"

For a moment she could say nothing. A bead of sweat rivered down between her breasts. A matching one rolled down Ty's throat. The insects buzzed lullingly. The faint breeze whispered through the feathery branches of the cypresses, but everything else was still, especially the stare that Sunny shared with Ty Beaumont.

"I think I'd really better go in now," she said at last. "I might get burned." She didn't mean it as a double entendre and hoped he didn't take it that way. It was difficult to tell exactly what his half-smile meant.

"George told me quite a story about you."

She hated him for bringing her past into their conversation. At the same time she thanked him. It served to yank her out of the muzzy state his deep voice had induced while talking about perfume and its application. Was she nuts? Why hadn't she gotten up and gone in? Maybe she *had* been in the sun too long.

"Was it true, Sunny?"

"That depends on what he told you, doesn't it?" she demanded sharply.

"He said you were one of the prettiest girls in school."

Sunny glanced away. "I guess I was well liked."

"Is that why you came back to Latham Green after four years of college?"

"My parents still lived here."

"Then. But not now."

"No, not now."

"Not since you marched out of the Baptist church and left your bridegroom standing at the altar."

Sunny glared at him. "Well, that answers my question. I see that George was talkative."

"Can you blame him? That's quite a story. I don't recall ever hearing about another bride who, when asked, 'Will you . . .' etcetera, said, 'No, I don't believe I will,' and turned on her heel and marched down the aisle and out of the church, leaving everybody, the bridegroom included, flabbergasted."

Sunny's cheeks were fiery and it had nothing to do with the slight sunburn she was getting. Memories overwhelmed her. Like quagmires in the nearby swamp, they had been concealed, waiting for her to slip and fall into them so they could suck her under and smother her.

"That took a lot of guts," Ty said, watching her closely.

She had thought he might laugh at her or joke about the bizarre way she had halted her wedding ceremony. Instead he looked almost commiserative. Well, she appreciated his not making fun of her, but she sure as hell didn't need his pity.

"I couldn't marry him."

"I don't think I could, either. If I were a woman, that is. Don Jenkins is as dry and crusty as yesterday's toast. He would never have satisfied a sensuous woman like you. He wouldn't even know where to start."

Scooting on his bottom, Ty moved closer to her. "It just seems to me that you would have known that before the preacher posed that all-important question. I mean, there you were in your long, white lace wedding dress."

"It was ecru," she corrected absently. Lost in

memory, she picked at the frayed hem of her beach towel.

"From what George told me, everybody in town was there."

"Yes."

"Why'd you do it, Sunny?"

Memories and lethargy were swept away by a sudden clarity. Her head snapped up. Her eyes were glowing like hot coals. "None of your damn business, Mr. Beaumont."

A laugh started as a low rumble deep in his chest. "And apparently nobody else's, either. To this day no one has figured it out. There's been speculation, of course."

"I'm sure there has been."

"Like a baby."

"*What*?" Sunny's breath rushed out. She had to drag it back before she could add, "They think I was pregnant?"

"According to George, that was everybody's first guess. You left because you couldn't bear the shame."

"Latham Green isn't that far behind the times. Lots of girls have been pregnant on their wedding day."

"But the babies belonged to the men they were marrying."

Sunny only stared at him in speechless amazement. "You mean everybody thought . . . " She couldn't even verbalize the scandalous idea.

Ty shrugged. "It was mentioned that the baby belonged to someone besides Don."

Disgusted with the fertile imaginations of small town minds, Sunny said, "There *was* no baby, for heaven's sake. Don's or anyone else's."

"I didn't think so. No stretch marks." Before she could prepare herself for it, he ran his finger over the taut skin of her lower abdomen. "Naturally I'd have to see your breasts to be positive."

Sunny retreated beyond his reach. "I've never had a baby," she ground out.

He poked the air with his index finger. "Now *that* was everyone's second theory. You were supposed to have a baby, but you didn't."

"An abortion?" Sunny, horrified by the thought, could barely breathe the word. "Everybody figured that I ran off to New Orleans to get an abortion?" She covered her face with her hands. "No wonder my parents had to leave." After a moment, she flung her head back and glared up at Ty. "Tell me the rest of it. What else do they say?"

"It gets real nasty from here."

"I want to know. Fran never would tell me what everybody said about me after I left. Tell me." He seemed reluctant. "Tell me," she repeated stubbornly.

He drew a deep breath. "Some thought you might have been on drugs."

"Ridiculous. What else?"

"VD was a consideration, but thought highly unlikely. Some thought you might like girls better than boys."

"You're kidding!"

"I'm only repeating what George said, you understand. The most popular theory, second to the baby one, was that you . . . uh . . . never mind."

"Come on, give."

"Nope, I gotta be going."

He made as if to rise. Sunny caught his arm. "Tell me, damn you. You brought this up."

His gaze moved slowly over her troubled face, taking in the messy ponytail on the top of her head and the curling tendrils which sweat had glued to her neck. It finally settled on her mouth. "Are you frigid, Sunny?"

Her hand fell from his arm. She stared up at

him in mute incredulity. "Just because I wouldn't marry Don, they think I'm frigid?"

He frowned and gave a dismissive shrug. "People talk. They make up things and twist them until the wild stories fit their own purposes." He peered at her closely. "Of course there's usually some basis for speculation."

"There's absolutely no basis for this speculation."

"George says you went through boyfriends like Kleenex."

"George is prone to exaggerate."

"Didn't you have a string of broken hearts to your credit?"

"I had my fair share of dates."

"Boys talk."

"Meaning?"

"According to George, no one ever claimed to . . . you know. You never . . ."

Sunny was fuming. "Went all the way?"

He flashed a fleeting, though dazzling, smile. "Quaint phrase, but that about sums it up, yes. From what I hear, you left the boys of Latham Green hot and bothered. You'd only go so far, then zip." He laughed at his own play on words. "I didn't mean that literally."

"Disgusting." Despite the heat, she shivered.

"Some unflattering names are pinned on girls who tease." His blue gaze moved over her. "Personally I don't believe it about you. But you've got to admit they have a good case. You're still single. You don't have any boyfriends."

"I have boyfriends!"

"How many?"

Sunny was immobilized when the realization struck her. She shot him a baleful look from beneath her brows, then gradually raised her head. Her golden eyes were smoldering. "You're making all this up, aren't you? Aren't you?" She surged to her feet. "You bastard." She aimed a kick at his shin, but he dodged it. "Get off my pier."

He sprang to his feet, reached for her and missed. "Just calm down."

"Calm down? Calm down!" She was so furious her voice squeaked. "I'm going to kill you. I have a gun in the cabin," she warned, pointing in that direction. "I'll shoot you if you don't get into that boat—"

"I only wanted to know who my competition was."

"You don't have any competition because you aren't even in the running."

"From my point of view it looks like you're leading me a merry chase."

"Tell it to the devil when you see him."

"Now, Sunny, is that nice? I wasn't making it *all* up. There *was* gossip about a baby and an abortion and all the rest." He lowered his head until his lips were moving only inches above hers. "I only added the part about you being frigid to see how you'd react." Smiling, he placed his hands on her shoulders. "You shot that theory all to hell. You're as hot as a firecracker."

"You'll never know, Mr. Beaumont."

"Don't be too sure. I want to win that wager. I like a glass of whiskey in the evening, especially when it's mixed with just enough water to make it the color of your eyes."

"Let go of me."

"I like the way it goes down." He pulled her closer. "Smooth and warm. I like when it hits my belly and spreads its heat."

Sunny's knees weren't making any guarantees that they could support her should he let go. On the contrary, they threatened to unhinge at any moment. Her senses were reeling. It was true that she had men friends who took her out to dinner and to the movies, a few of whom she would invite in for drinks and some harmless necking.

But never in her life had she met a man who turned her inside out just by what he said and the suggestive way he said it. The men she went out with were unremarkable and forgettable. Once she bade a date good-night, she rarely remembered what he had worn or what his cologne had smelled like.

Ty Beaumont wouldn't be so easily forgotten. His hard frame was imprinting itself on the front of her body, stamping an impression so deep that even when it was no longer there she knew she would feel it. The smell of his skin would tantalize her memory forever.

That didn't prove that she wanted him. It only proved that she was alive. Because only a female corpse could resist this inundation of masculinity.

"Even if I hadn't bet a case of whiskey on it, I'd still want to take you to bed, Sunny Chandler. You're just as intoxicating."

"I won't stand here and—"

"Good idea."

Before she knew what was happening, she was sitting on the towel again. Ty was on his knees, straddling her thighs and supporting her head with his strong hands.

When she saw his mouth descending toward hers, she turned her head away. "No!"

He inclined his head back. "Maybe I was right. Maybe you can't stand a man's touch."

"That's not true."

"Well then . . ."

Sunny flopped down on the bed.

The cold shower hadn't helped. Lowering the air conditioner's thermostat hadn't helped. Turning on the rotating fan overhead hadn't helped.

She was hot.

She had adjusted the shutters on the window to allow only narrow stripes of sunlight through. The bedroom, which had always been hers when her family used the cabin, should have been cool by now. Instead she felt as if it were stifling and she was on fire.

Impatient with the heat, she sat up and whipped the nightgown over her head and tossed it on the rocking chair beside the bed. She had put the nightie on after her shower because it was the coolest garment she owned. The white lawn didn't touch anywhere except the shoulder straps . . . except for today. This afternoon it seemed to cling to her like an affectionate ghost.

And, just as tenaciously, her mind clung to the memory of that hateful kiss.

She hadn't responded.

"I didn't," she hissed at the ceiling, as though to convince it of what she hadn't been able to persuade herself.

His mouth had been so unapologetically hungry, so consummately male, as it moved over hers. He had pressed his lips determinedly against hers until they had parted. Then—

Sunny groaned. Her stomach went weightless and her womanhood blossomed with a pulsing warmth when she recalled his tongue sleekly thrusting its way between her lips and into her mouth. Undisciplined. Erotic. Such a thief. Because it had robbed her of the will to resist.

At that moment she had stopped trying to squirm away from him. The bones in her neck had turned to jelly. Her head had fallen back even more, giving him freer access to her mouth. Again and again his tongue had penetrated, delving deeper each time.

She had allowed it! Heaven forbid, she had even encouraged it, reaching for his tongue with her own when his withdrew.

With her capitulation, his hold had gentled. The hands, which had been firmly cupping the back of her head, moved down to her neck. His fingers stroked her nape with the same loving tenderness that his lips pressed soft kisses onto hers.

"My fingers are still oily," he had whispered. "Think how good it would feel if I . . ."

Sunny looked down at her body now and saw that her nipples were responding with the recollection just as they had at his breathtaking suggestions. When he had whispered in that devil's voice of his about what he would like to do with his lips and tongue, her breasts had ached with longing for him to stop talking about it and start doing it.

Sunny shuddered. Her skin was finally cooling off. She had goose bumps. But the fire inside her still raged out of control. It was a conflagration of humiliation as much as desire.

"Damn him."

She had repeated the curse a thousand times. For at the moment when she was the most malleable, willing to participate in enacting the fantasies he whispered about, he had eased her back, smiled, and said, "I've stayed too long. I've got to go."

As she watched, trembling with remnant desire and rage, he had hopped down into his boat. As he unwound the rope from the pile he said, "I'd be careful sitting out here like that if I were you. There's all kinds of wackos prowling these woods, and your nearest neighbor lives over a mile away."

She had followed the direction of his gaze down and, to her further mortification, discovered that their embrace had worked down the top of her bikini. The creamy tops of her breasts were swelling out of it. She viciously tugged it back into place.

He winked audaciously a second before he replaced his sunglasses. "I'll be seeing you later, Sunny."

Then with a jaunty wave, he had left.

Sunny pulled the sheet over her nakedness, rolled to her side, and squeezed her eyes shut. She'd feel better after a nap. Maybe she was in the middle of a nap already and would soon wake up to discover that her visit from Ty Beaumont had been only a bad dream.

His taste lingered on her lips and tongue. She could still feel him, full and firm, pressing against the cradle of her femininity. His denim shorts had felt so good against her bare thighs. The ragged fringe had tickled. Her breasts flushed with heat and tingled with sensations every time his evocative words echoed in the chambers of her mind.

She hated him.

She woke up hours later, disoriented and uncomfortable. She stretched her cramped muscles. Her skin felt tight and was stinging from overexposure to the sun.

She got out of bed and pulled the nightgown back on. Her growling stomach reminded her that she hadn't eaten anything since the grapefruit this morning. She padded into the kitchen and cooked herself an omelet. Maybe tomorrow evening she'd eat dinner out. But she didn't feel like facing people tonight. Not if everything Ty Beaumont had said was true.

Had people who had known her all her life really thought those terrible things about her? No wonder they had stared at her last night at the party as though she were a freak.

And by going into town, she ran the risk of seeing Don and Gretchen. She couldn't bear that.

She cleaned up her few dishes and switched out the kitchen light. There was nothing to do until she grew sleepy again but read or watch television. She was trying to decide which when she heard the noise outside.

Three

Old houses settled and made creaking noises, right?

Right.

Branches knocked against the eaves when the wind blew, right?

Right.

So there was no need to panic, right?

Wrong. Because the noise was coming from the shed behind the house where her father used to clean fish. It couldn't have been made by settling timber or by the wind.

Sunny's heart was pounding so loudly that she thought she might have imagined the whole thing. But when she heard the noise again, like something or someone stamping through the underbrush behind the shed, she broke out in a cold sweat of fear.

Thankfully she realized she had already turned off the light in the kitchen. She crept toward the window over the sink, which afforded a view of the back of the property all the way down to the dock and the lake beyond. Her hand was shaking when she moved the curtain aside, creating a crack no wider than an inch, but wide enough for her to peek through.

Nothing. It was a dark night. There was only a partial moon, and it was obscured by clouds. The wind had picked up. The lake was choppier than it had been earlier in the day. It looked as though the clouds on the horizon might produce a summer storm after all.

Sunny stood motionless at the window for several minutes. Nothing beyond it stirred, except for the trees that bent gracefully in the wind. What she had heard must have been just blowing branches. She let the curtain fall back into place.

Shaking her head, amused and irritated with herself for behaving so foolishly, she turned and started to go out of the kitchen for the second time. Again, she got no farther than the doorway when she heard another noise. This time metal clanking against metal. Her father had stored buckets, gardening tools, and hardware out in the shed.

"Oh, dear God." Whimpering in fright, she mashed her fingers against her lips.

Steve and Fran had expressed concern about her staying alone out here at the lake.

"Nothing really criminal has happened out there," Steve had told her, "but kids have beer busts, get drunk, raise a little hell."

"Are you sure you wouldn't rather stay in town with me?" Fran had asked.

"Don't be silly. Your house will be in a state of chaos all week. I'll be safer alone at the lake."

Sunny regretted her decision now. If she hadn't been so stubborn, she could have been safely ensconced in the guest bedroom of Fran's house instead of shivering in fear in an isolated cabin.

She didn't waste another second, but hastened to the wall telephone, which her parents had never had disconnected. In the darkness, she overturned a kitchen chair. She stubbed her toe against the table as she lunged for the telephone receiver. She dialed O and waited breathlessly for the operator to answer.

The moment she answered, Sunny said, "I need help." Her words were hushed as they tumbled, one over the next, out of her trembling lips. She was certain she sounded hysterical and out of her senses, but she couldn't help it. "Call the police. Tell them to come right away. I'm alone and someone is outside my cabin at the lake. I think he might be trying to break in."

Although that wasn't quite true, it was better to be safe than sorry. Better to anticipate the criminal than to stand by and wait for him to make his move. Besides, it added an element of urgency to her message. It worked. Without hesitation the operator said, "I'm calling the sheriff's office right now. Someone will be there soon."

Sunny provided her with the rural address and hung up. Who else could she call? Her neighbors? She didn't know them. Not even by name. They had moved in since she had left town. Steve and Fran? Yes. If this were a false alarm, she'd feel really stupid, but . . .

The consequences of having false courage were too gruesome to think about. She bungled the series of memorized numbers twice before the call to Fran's house went through. The phone rang and rang while Sunny muttered, "Come on, come on, answer." When it became apparent that no one was there, she hung up, almost in tears now.

What if he were out there watching her through the window?

She almost collapsed when she recalled a previous conversation. "You should have become a window peeper." "How do you know I'm not?"

Good Lord! *He* was the one who had warned her about wackos roaming around the lake. *He* was the one who had pointed out that her nearest neighbor was over a mile away. *He* was the one who had gone to the trouble to find out where she was staying. *He* was the one who had crossed the lake to see her. And hadn't his final words—"I'll be seeing you later, Sunny"—carried both a promise and a threat?

What did she know about him? Nothing except his name. He had been invited to the wedding party, but serial killers were often charming men who lured their victims—

Stop it! Get control of yourself. Think of something constructive to do. Don't panic.

What was George Henderson's number? She'd call and ask him about this Ty Beaumont. But what was George's telephone number?

The drawer beneath the telephone was stuck. Sunny tried it several times, then tugged on it so hard that it came out of its moorings and crashed to the floor. The Latham Parish telephone directory, a few unsharpened pencils, a scrap of fabric her mother had used to match paint, a coupon for buy-one-catfish-dinner-get-one-free, and a rusty nail all scattered over the linoleum floor.

The racket she had made stunned her for a moment. Recovering, she dropped to her knees, gouging one on the head of the nail. She picked up the telephone book. As yet unaware that she couldn't read it in the dark, she began frantically thumbing through the old, curled pages.

It was then that she heard the heavy footsteps on the porch outside. She clutched the directory to her thudding heart. Her eyes were round with terror. She made a helpless mewing sound when the front doorknob rattled, as though someone was trying to open it.

She used the countertop to pull herself up. Her entire body was quaking with fear. Moving along the wall, she edged her way into the living room and stared in horror as the doorknob twisted first one way, then the other.

Sunny almost jumped out of her skin when the loud knock came. She hadn't expected the intruder to knock. She waited, but there was another knock, then another, becoming impatient and as hard and dramatic as her beating heart.

How unlike a window peeper or serial killer to announce his arrival. But who else could it be?

The sheriff, of course! Why hadn't she thought of that? She raced to the door, flipped up the lock, and breathlessly flung it open.

Ty Beaumont was standing on the threshold.

Sunny screamed.

Spinning around, she went racing back across the living room, intent on getting into her bedroom, which had a lock on the door.

She was brought up short when he grabbed a handful of her nightgown. "What the hell is wrong with you?" He whipped her around and brought her up hard against him. "Are you all right? What's happened?"

"I've called the sheriff," she said in loud defiance.

"You have?"

"Yes. He's on his way. He'll be here any minute."

"He's already here." His lips twitched with the need to smile. Then he mimicked her gape-mouthed expression of incredulity.

"You're—"

"Sheriff Ty Beaumont. Pleased to make your acquaintance, ma'am," he drawled in a broad Southwestern accent. "How can I be of service?"

"By going straight to hell!"

Sunny shoved herself away from him, seething

with anger over his amusement, which he didn't have the good manners to hide. Actually Sunny was just as angry with herself as she was with him. She, who had lived alone in New Orleans for years, had let her imagination run away with her and had behaved like a complete fool. He would think she was an idiot.

With a broad sweep of her hand, she pushed her tangled hair back. "How do I know you're the sheriff?"

With that same drawl and the lowering of one eyelid, he said, "Wanna see my pistol?"

Macy's Thanksgiving Day Parade was more subtle than his innuendo. Her eyes became slits of fury. "Why didn't you tell me?"

"Did you ask?"

"What were you doing sneaking around my house in the middle of the night?"

"I was responding to your call for help. Arleta, the operator, said you sounded scared out of your wits."

"I was!"

"Are you always such a 'fraidy cat?"

"Of course not. What were you doing out in the shed?"

"What shed?"

"You mean that wasn't *you*?"

"You mean there really *was* a suspicious noise?"

"Why else would I call?" Sunny cried.

He hooked his thumbs beneath the waistband of his tight jeans and cocked his head to one side. "I figured that you invented this 'intruder' just to get me out here."

"You arrogant sonofa—" Rage flickered like flames in her eyes. "I heard something out in the shed," she said, pointing in the direction of the kitchen.

A deep crease of genuine worry formed between

his brows. "Then I'd better take a look. You stay here."

Disobeying, she followed him into the kitchen on tiptoes. She watched as he opened the back door, unlatched the screen, and stepped through it. The moon cast enough light to make him a tall silhouette as he crossed the yard. He had brought a flashlight with him and turned it on, shining it into the dense forest that surrounded the cabin. When her father bought the property, he had cleared only enough land to build the cabin. By design they had left the wooded lot as virgin as possible.

From behind the screen door, Sunny watched Beaumont disappear around the far side of the shed. She could see the flashlight's beam arcing over the pier and through the trees. It seemed to take forever before he came back into view. He switched off the flashlight before reentering the kitchen.

She moved aside, holding the screen door open for him. "Well?"

"You had intruders all right."

"Intruders, plural?"

"Four," he said grimly.

Her face paled. "Four."

"Yep, a mama raccoon and three babies."

Sunny opened her mouth to speak, decided that anything she said would only make her look more ridiculous, and shut her mouth quickly. Her teeth clicked together in the sudden silence.

"They were stashing leftovers behind a row of buckets," he told her. She kept her head down and could all but feel his damned blue eyes boring a hole into the top of it. The thought of him laughing at her was untenable.

She raised her head suddenly. "It's partially your

fault," she shouted accusingly. "All that talk about window peepers and wackos."

"You brought up the window peepers, not me." He casually laid his flashlight on the kitchen table. "Got a cup of coffee?"

"No."

She could see his wide smile in the darkness. "Not even for the trooper who rescued you from a family of rampaging raccoons?"

She planted her fists on her hips. "You're enjoying this, aren't you?"

He righted the chair she had overturned and plopped down in it, sitting more on his spine than his bottom. He grinned up at her. "Well, you gotta admit that the scenery is breathtaking."

When Sunny realized that she had nothing on but the scanty nightgown and that her stance was stretching the sheer cloth tightly across her breasts, her arms dropped to her sides. She spun around and went charging out of the kitchen.

The mess from the drawer lay directly in her path of retreat. She broke one of the pencils under her foot, while her other heel made contact with the head of the nail. Cursing in a most unladylike fashion, she hobbled out of the kitchen.

Minutes later she returned dressed in a tank T-shirt and a pair of shorts. The light in the kitchen was on and Ty already had a pot of coffee perking on the gas range.

"Make yourself at home."

Ignoring her sarcasm, he replied, "Thanks, I already did."

She went to the cabinet and began taking down cups and saucers. "Cream and sugar?"

"Black's fine. Got any cookies?"

She rolled her eyes ceilingward and produced a package of cookies from the pantry, which she had stocked for her week's stay.

"Just for the record," he mumbled around a big bite of chocolate-frosted cookie, "I liked the other outfit better."

"No doubt."

"Although this one has distinct possibilities."

On the word "distinct," his eyes slid down to her breasts. It was evident that she wasn't wearing a bra under the soft knit fabric that molded to her figure. The longer he looked at her, the more evident it became.

Sunny tried to cover her discomfiture with a snide question. "Do the taxpayers of Latham Green have any idea that their sheriff is a sex fiend?"

He chuckled. "I'm on duty."

"Somehow I don't find that very reassuring."

"Well, you should. If I weren't on duty, I'd have you in bed by now."

"Not a chance, Mr. Beaumont."

His grin reeked of self-confidence. "It's ready." He grinned wickedly at her start of surprise. "The coffee, Sunny. The *coffee* is ready."

She poured, trying not to think about him looking at the bare backs of her thighs, which she was certain he was doing. "How long have you been sheriff?" she asked, setting a full cup of coffee in front of him.

"Since I got here. I moved here specifically to take the job."

"And before that?" She sat down across from him and sipped her coffee.

For the first time since he'd asked her to dance the night before, his eyes stopped smiling. In fact, they turned hard and cold. The deep vertical clefts on both sides of his mouth no longer resembled laugh lines. "Before that I was somewhere else."

"Oh."

Sunny got the message. His past wasn't open

for review. She envied him that. She wished hers wasn't. In New Orleans she was safe. No one knew about the debacle with Don Jenkins. Her friends there knew she had moved to the city from a small town, but no one had ever pressed her for information about herself. She appreciated that.

That's why she honored Ty Beaumont's need for privacy now, even though he was the most aggravating man she'd ever met. She refrained from asking him any probing questions and filled the yawning silence by nibbling on a cookie.

He was the first to speak. "Did you have an accident?"

Sunny followed the jutting motion of his chin down to the floor, where the debris from the drawer was still scattered. She laughed with self-derision. "I was going to look up George Henderson's telephone number and check you out."

"He would have felt obliged to give you a glowing report. He works for me."

"George is a law officer?"

"My deputy."

Sunny shook her head with disbelief. "I remember when he stole watermelons."

"I think he still does."

They laughed together, and it felt good. A little too good for Sunny to feel truly comfortable about it. When their laughter subsided, she realized just how intimate the setting and situation were. "It's getting late." She practically snatched Ty's coffee cup away from him and carried it along with hers to the sink.

"Are you limping?"

"It's nothing," she said with a negligent shrug as she replaced the package of cookies in the pantry.

"It's something."

She lifted her foot off the floor, holding her leg out straight at a thirty-degree angle. "My knee found the head of that nail when I went down on all fours. See?" She indicated the tiny red mark on her knee. "Nothing to it."

"That's not enough to make you limp."

"I stubbed my toe, too."

"What else?"

"Nothing," she stressed.

"What?" Though Ty spoke the question softly, it conveyed his determination to get the truth from her.

"I stepped on the damn nail," she cried in frustration. "Okay?"

"Not okay. Sit." He sternly pointed at the chair she had vacated.

"It's time you left, Sheriff."

"If you don't let me check your foot, I'll feel that it's my professional duty to take you to the hospital. Then the whole story about the raccoons and the window-peeper scare will be the topic of conversation at the beauty parlor tomorrow and—"

Sunny's fanny landed hard in the chair.

"That's better," Ty said, and smiled. "Give me your foot."

She didn't actually offer her foot for his inspection. He bent forward and picked it up off the floor, unbalancing her so that her bottom slid almost to the rim of her seat. Bracing herself in the chair with stiff arms and hands that curled over the edge of the chair, she watched as his large, tanned hands enfolded her foot.

He turned it up and examined the sole. "Here?" He touched the crescent-shaped wound on her heel. She winced. "Sore?"

"With you mashing on it, it is."

"Helluva bruise. You're lucky it didn't break the skin. Almost, but not quite. You don't need a tetanus shot, but you might want to watch it for the next few days."

"I will. Thanks." She tried to pull her foot away, but to no avail. He closed his hands around it, enclosing it firmly and snugly between his palms.

"They're a little skinny, but otherwise you have very nice feet."

"Is this part of your official duty, Sheriff Beaumont?"

"My duty is to aid and abet the citizens of Latham Parish. Right now, I think this citizen needs a foot rub."

She squirmed in her chair when his thumb drew a sizzling line down the center of her sole. In a bizarre and titillating correlation, the caress tickled the back of her throat.

"I was in Japan once." He brushed his thumb over her toes and examined each glossy toenail. "They give fantastic foot rubs there. This geisha—"

"I'm really not interested."

"—used a lot of lotion on her hands. Got any?"

"We'll do without."

"Suit yourself. Anyway, this geisha had a way of squeezing each individual toe between her fingers. Hard, but not enough to hurt. Kinda like sucking."

He matched action to words by wringing Sunny's middle toe between his strong fingers. She felt the caress in every other part of her body, especially the erogenous ones. The caress even looked erotic. The backs of his fingers were sprinkled with fine blond hairs. His hands looked dark, manly, and masterful against her slender foot.

In quick succession, forbidden sensations rippled out of Sunny's middle. When he massaged the base of each toe on the underside of her foot, she almost sprang out of her chair. "I don't think this is proper."

He grinned unrepentantly. "I bet it isn't. But it sure as hell feels good, doesn't it? Let's treat ourselves. After all, you suffered a scare and I saved your life. I think we're due some R and R. I won't tell if you won't."

Sunny found his coaxing voice and bedroom expression almost as hypnotic as the foot massage. She offered no resistance when he wedged her heel into the notch between his thighs.

"Then this geisha, after milking each muscle and bone in my foot, massaged only the very tips of my toes. Like this. Tiny circles. Sometimes so light I thought I was imagining her touch."

Sunny actually gasped at the startling sensations that shot like rockets up her leg. Reflexively, her foot moved, pressing itself more firmly against his fly. She dared not think of what was filling her high arch.

"Of course they say," Ty continued in that mesmerizing voice, "that the most delicious sensation is to have them tongued."

Sunny's eyes slid closed.

The next thing she knew she was catching herself to keep from falling off her chair. He had peremptorily lowered her foot back to the floor and was dusting his hands as though he had just completed a chore.

"But tonguing cost extra and I was just a poor G.I. low on cash, so I can't claim to have experienced that particular pleasure firsthand. Can you?" he asked guilelessly.

Furious over her own culpability, Sunny bounded out of her chair and said coldly, "It's time you left."

Past time. Way past time, she was thinking. Was she crazy, allowing him to touch her like that? Talk to her so outrageously? She stamped out of the kitchen, turning on lights as she went.

She wanted to fill the cabin up with light, noise, anything to dispel the pervasive aura of privacy.

"Thank you for coming." By the time he followed her into the common room, she was already at the front door, ungraciously holding it open for him.

"That's what they pay me for."

"How did you get here so fast anyway?"

"I was already here."

"Already here?"

He nodded. "I had driven out to check on you."

"Why, for heaven's sake?"

"I got worried about those wackos, too."

"There weren't any wackos."

"But we didn't know that for sure. And if you couldn't handle a family of raccoons, how do you think you'd stand up against a wacko?"

"Good night, Mr. Beaumont."

"I was almost here when they radioed my patrol car that you suspected a prowler and needed help. Didn't you see my headlights?"

Feeling the greater fool, she avoided his mocking eyes. "No, I didn't. I was in the kitchen. Now I feel all safe and sound, knowing that you're patrolling the lake."

"Why did you panic when you heard the noise? Why didn't you just get your gun?"

"Gun?"

"The one you threatened to shoot me with this afternoon if I didn't get off your dock."

"I didn't—my father probably took it when . . . I don't know where . . . It wasn't loaded."

"What is this, multiple choice?"

She glared at him.

"Are you sure there *was* a gun?"

"Good night, Mr. Beaumont," she repeated through clenched teeth.

"What's all this?"

Ty's attention had been attracted to the table, where several sketch pads were spread out. The pencil sketches were, for the most part, unfinished.

Sunny sighed heavily, making no effort to conceal her annoyance. She slammed the open front door closed because it was letting mosquitoes in. "Drawings."

"Bugs?" he asked, holding up one of her sketches and eyeing it critically.

"It's a dragonfly."

"Dragonflies again. Are they your hobby or something? You're not a very good artist," he remarked candidly.

She yanked the sketch away from him and returned it to the table. "And you're not a very good sheriff. You don't even wear a uniform."

He was dressed in jeans and a plain white shirt, which looked anything but plain on him. The sleeves were rolled up his forearms to just below his elbows. The white cotton set off his deep tan and piercing blue eyes. It even matched the smile he flashed down at her.

"But I've got a silver badge and a patrol car with flashing lights. If you're nice I'll take you for a ride in it sometime."

"I doubt that being nice would win a woman any points with you, Mr. Beaumont."

He tipped his head toward her as though to say, "Score one for you." Still, his smile wasn't one of contrition. He had almost reached the door when he stopped abruptly, snapped his fingers, and said, "Oops, forgot my flashlight." He retraced his steps into the kitchen.

Sunny waited by the front door. What was taking so long? she wondered, when a minute passed and he didn't reappear. "Mr. Beaumont?" she called. Nothing. Impatiently, she tapped her bare foot against the floor.

Another minute went by and he still didn't come back. Curious and vexed, Sunny went into the kitchen after him. She found him leaning against the countertop studying his wristwatch.

"What on earth are you doing?"

"Come here," he said, keeping his eyes on the face of his watch.

Intrigued, she padded over to the counter and joined him in watching his wristwatch. It wasn't doing anything out of the ordinary, certainly nothing so captivating as to absorb him this way. The second hand was sweeping its way up toward the twelve.

"Five, four, three, two, one," Ty said, counting down.

"So? What does that mean?"

"That means, Sunny Chandler, that you're in serious trouble."

He turned, and by doing so, pinned her in the corner where the cabinets met and blocked off her escape with his body. He braced his hands on both sides of her hips and leaned into her. "It's midnight."

"Is this where you turn back into a rat?"

He laughed. "In a manner of speaking. I'm officially off duty."

She glowered at his grinning face. "Get away from me."

"Ah, come on, Sunny. Be a sport." He took a strand of her hair between his fingers and whisked it back and forth across her neck. "I just got off work after a hard day. I had to break up a fight between two dads at the Little League ballgame, track down a lost kid, and arrest a guy for DWI. Not to mention patrolling the riotous streets of Latham Green and rescuing a hysterical woman from a herd of raccoons. Or is it a pack of raccoons?" He shrugged. "Anyway, you get my drift.

It's time to play. Don't you want to play with me?"

"No. And will you—" Her sentence ended on a gasp of surprise. "What are you doing?"

"Feeling your heart." He laid his hand over the top curve of her breast. "When I came in, I could see your pulse pounding. Here." He pressed her breast. "And here." He settled his lips against the base of her throat and planted a sweet kiss there. "Know what?" He slid his hand just inside her tank top. "I think it's pounding just as hard now."

Not only was her heart pounding, but her breath was coming in shallow pants that pushed her breast up into his curving palm. He didn't move his hand, didn't claim more than that upper curve. Her nipple tightened in preparation for a caress that never came. It was maddening.

"Leave me alone." Sunny's voice was feeble and lacked conviction. But how could she possibly muster imperiousness when he was taking love bites up and down her throat?

"Want to know a secret?" His lips moved beneath her hair to her ear. "When I saw you standing in the doorway wearing nothing but that nightie, my heart started pounding, too. Feel it."

With his free hand, he lifted hers. He tucked it inside his shirt, directly over his heart. The steady, solid beat filled her hand. The warm skin was as comfortable as a fireplace on a frosty morning. The forest of hair prompted curious explorations from her fingers.

His teeth closed gently on her earlobe. He worried the two diamond studs with the tip of his tongue. "After I left this afternoon, did you think about me?"

"No."

"Liar." He nudged her thighs apart and cushioned himself in that warm, soft cove. "You thought about me. About us. Together. You thought about that kiss."

"No, no, I didn't."

His laughter was husky and deep. "Oh, yes, you did. That's all I thought about. I was almost derelict in my duties thinking about that kiss." His mouth moved back to hers. He rubbed her lips with his. "My tongue inside your mouth. Moving in and out. Just like making love."

"Stop it." The protest was little more than a ragged breath.

"No way, Sunny. Not until you're beneath me. Naked. Wanting."

He kissed her again. As before, the world as she knew it crumbled. She was transported into a sphere where everything smelled and tasted and felt like Ty. It was his universe. He dominated it, was lord over it.

He moved his hand down a fraction. His fingers impressed tunnels into the fullness of her breast, but he still ignored the crest, which was yearning, aching, for his touch.

Her fingers curled into the hard flesh of his chest. Her mouth responded to the expert probing of his tongue. Involuntarily she moved her hips, bringing his hardness fully against her. The contact shocked them both.

His eyes were dark and intense when he raised his head and looked down into her face. Her lips were rosy and wet. She stared back at him with lambent eyes.

"But as you've already pointed out," he said quietly, "it's getting late."

Sunny couldn't believe it!

He calmly released her and left the kitchen. Moments later she heard the front door close and then the motor of a car starting up. By the time she had recovered herself, he was gone.

Sunny Chandler shattered the cup he had drunk from against her kitchen wall and called upon every demon in hell to possess the body and soul of Ty Beaumont.

Four

Sunny crossed her legs, demurely tugging her straight skirt over her knees when she noticed that her impatient movement had attracted the attention of the man behind the desk.

"The financial statement is as complete as I could make it, Mr. Smithie. I've included several credit references, my income tax records for the past three years, my projections for future income."

"You've been thorough, Miss Chandler."

That gave Sunny no indication of what the bank officer thought of the columns of figures he had perused no less than a dozen times since she'd arrived fifteen minutes earlier. Peering through his bifocals, he scanned the pages again.

Then he set aside the meticulously prepared financial statement, folded his hands on his desk, and looked at Sunny as though he was about to impart the sad news that there was no Santa Claus. His expression was that superior, that remorseful, that sympathetic. She braced herself for having her high hopes dashed against the rocks of sexual prejudice.

"The figures you submitted are impressive, Miss Chandler."

"But realistic, I believe." She smiled, trying not to let her trepidation show. Banks didn't lend money to people who looked like they needed it.

"Much as I admire your enthusiasm for your work, I'm afraid you're being a trifle optimistic."

"On the contrary, I've been conservative in my projections."

"Still," Mr. Smithie said, clearing his throat importantly, "they're only projections."

"Projections based on experience." At the risk of being argumentative, Sunny wouldn't take no for an answer without putting up a good fight. "I know what women, and men for that matter, are prepared to spend on these things. My clients will be society people with staggering incomes."

"But you have no clients at present," he pointed out reasonably.

"That's why I need the business loan, Mr. Smithie. To promote my new business. I *do* have clients, people who will work only with me where I am currently employed. They won't hear of entrusting themselves to anyone else. Once they know I'm in business for myself, they'll naturally come to me."

He looked skeptical, but didn't offer a rebuttal. Instead he glanced down at his wristwatch, a reminder that she was taking up a great deal of his valuable time. "As for collateral—"

"The lake property."

"But that actually belongs to your father."

"And you have in the file a letter authorizing me to use it. Do you think I forged his signature on the letter, Mr. Smithie?"

"Of course not, Sunny," he said with a falsely jovial smile. He had lapsed into using her first name. Neither of them noticed because at any other time prior to today, he'd always called her Sunny.

"Then I fail to see the problem. The value of the lake cabin and surrounding acreage more than covers the amount I'm asking to borrow. As you know, my father is a respected businessman. He wouldn't risk his property if he didn't believe in what I want to do."

"But going into business for oneself," he said with a mournful shake of his head, "that's an ambitious undertaking for anybody. But especially for a woman."

Sunny sat back in her chair and eyed him assessingly. "You mean that if I were a man, the bank would have no qualms about lending me the money?"

He held up both hands. "No, no, not at all. The bank has no such prejudices."

I'll just bet, Sunny thought.

"It's simply that most of the young ladies who grow up here get married and . . ." Too late Mr. Smithie realized his faux pas. The deepening color in his cheeks did Sunny a world of good. Now she had him on the defensive. "What I mean to say is, it would make better sense if you applied for a loan at a bank in New Orleans."

She had. She had applied at several banks and been turned down. The Latham Green National Bank was her last hope, but she didn't want Mr. Smithie to know that. "I thought you would appreciate my business," she said with a saucy smile.

"Oh, we do, we do, it's just . . ." He foundered, shuffling papers on his desk while he searched for something to say. She almost felt sorry for him. He wanted to turn her down in a way that would spare her, him, and the bank any awkwardness. He probably wished she hadn't been his first client on this Monday morning. Helluva way to launch the week.

Well, fine, she thought. *Welcome to the club, Mr. Smithie.*

Her week hadn't started out so great, either. First, she'd had to return to a town she had thought she'd seen the last of. Then she'd fallen prey to that crocodile-cum-sheriff. At the stroke of midnight last night she'd found out just how dangerous an animal he was.

Thinking about him only fueled her determination to make this necessary trip to Latham Green pay off. She leaned forward and spoke in a whisper that intimated urgency. "Mr. Smithie, forget for a minute that you've known me since I was in diapers. Forget that I'm female and single and a woman on my own. Just listen to me." She wet her lips. "I need that loan. I want to go into business for myself. Without this loan I can't. My father's credit was always good at this bank. Mine will be, too. You won't be taking a risk."

He pursed his pale banker's lips. "You force me to be blunt, Sunny. The bank takes pride in lending money to energetic young people with ambition. But we are careful to make certain that they demonstrate sound judgment and a sense of responsibility. And frankly . . . to be honest . . . well . . . what you did . . ."

She flopped back in her chair and stared at him, aghast. "What I did three years ago demonstrates a lack of sound judgment and sense of responsibility. Is that it?"

By way of answer, he lowered his gaze to the polished surface of his desk.

Sunny raised a hand to her forehead and rubbed the center of it where she was developing a splitting headache. She'd anticipated—feared, dreaded—being turned down, but not because of her aborted marriage to Don Jenkins.

Was that to haunt her for the rest of her life? Didn't people realize that for her to have done it, she must have had an extremely good reason? Did everyone think it was a spur-of-the-moment decision, some flight of whimsy?

"Perhaps a smaller amount," Mr. Smithie said in conciliation for having been so hurtfully blunt.

Sunny was adamantly shaking her head before he even finished. "I'll be dealing with people who only go first class. *I* have to be top drawer, cream of the crop, elite. If I start cutting corners right off the bat, I'll be dead before I even start."

He pulled on his cheek. "Perhaps if we review your situation—"

"I haven't got the luxury of time. I have to do it now."

"But Mardi Gras is a long way off. Not until next spring."

"They start making plans months in advance. I've got to start right away or wait another year." She laid her hands flat on his desk. "I know what you and everybody else in town think of me because of what happened on my wedding day, but I'm damn good at what I do." She slapped the surface of his desk for emphasis. His eyebrows shot up. At least she had his attention. "I'm going to make a lot of money in the next few years. I'd like to deposit some of it in this bank. Yes or no, Mr. Smithie? I need your answer. Otherwise you're wasting my time."

He was no longer looking at her as though she was the only tryout who hadn't made the team. Instead, his implacable eyes sparked with a flicker of interest and respect.

"I'll reconsider your application and speak with

the other loan officers. Come back one week from today and I'll let you know."

"Not good enough. I'm leaving next Sunday morning. I need to know by Friday at the latest."

He considered her a moment longer. "I'll see what I can do, but I'm making you no promises." He stood up, indicating that her claim on his time had expired. When Sunny shook his hand, she was glad to note that his was just as damp as hers. He would probably turn down her application, but at least she had made an impression on him.

She slid on a pair of sunglasses as she walked through the bank's austere lobby, telling herself that the glasses weren't a means of avoiding the curious glances she intercepted.

Stepping outside was like walking into a sauna. The heat was humid and, today, oppressive. Even with sunglasses on it took a moment for her eyes to adjust to the glaring light that only a partly cloudy day in the South in the summer could produce. When her eyes did acclimatize, she groaned at what she saw.

Ty Beaumont was leaning against the wall of the bank. One knee was bent, his booted foot resting flat against the bricks. A straw cowboy hat was pulled down low over his brows. His thumbs were hooked in the belt loops of his jeans. If it hadn't been for the leather holster around his hips and the silver badge on the breast pocket of his white shirt, one would have thought he was a loafer instead of a law officer.

Since her car was parked in the next block, she had no choice but to walk past him or go completely around the city block. It was too hot for that long a hike. Getting past him unseen was out of the question, and, since she didn't want to be put on the defensive, she was the first to speak.

"Expecting a bank holdup?"

He grinned, splitting his face into a visage far too handsome for his own good. He should pose for one of those macho cigarette ads, Sunny thought. He was certainly the type, having just enough character lines to make his face ruggedly appealing.

"Never can tell," he said, lazily pushing himself away from the wall and falling into step beside her. "It would sure liven up an otherwise sluggish Monday morning."

"Trust me, the bank is carefully guarding its money."

"Oh?"

"Never mind. That subject is closed."

"Okay. Then may I say that you look as fresh as a sprig of mint this morning, Miss Sunny." He had assumed the role of a Southern gentleman as they strolled past the storefronts.

Taking up her cue, Sunny replied flirtatiously, "Thank you, sir, but I'm afraid I'll soon wilt in this stiflin' heat."

"Maybe you should have brought a fan."

"I didn't have one to go with this outfit."

She wasn't the business suit type, but had dressed in keeping with her appointment with Mr. Smithie. The crisp green linen dress, which she had accessorized with white shoes and jewelry, was tailored but cool, fashionable but not funky. Funky wouldn't have done at all in the Latham Green National Bank. "Maybe it'll rain soon and cool things off."

"Are we already reduced to talking about the weather?"

"We don't have to talk about anything. I'll say goodbye here." They were at the center of downtown, waiting at the intersection for one of the few traffic lights in town to change.

"I'm going this way anyway," he said casually.

He took her elbow to assist her as she stepped off the uneven sidewalk onto the rutted pavement of the street which, when wearing high heels, was treacherous. "Did you recover from our kiss last night?" She kept her eyes trained on the pavement, saying nothing. "Is that subject closed, too?" he asked.

"Yes."

"All right. Can I buy you a cup of coffee?"

"No, thank you."

"Cherry Coke?"

"No, I've—"

"Humor me. This Woolworth's still makes the best cherry Cokes in the world. That's one of Latham Green's few claims to fame."

Again he took her elbow and, to avoid causing a scene that would no doubt entertain the passersby, Sunny had no choice but to go along when he pulled her through the door of the variety store.

Entering it was like stepping back in time. The same fans circulated overhead even though the store had installed central air conditioning years ago. The wooden floors still creaked in the same places and smelled pleasantly of the lemon oil with which they were dust-mopped. The shelves were stocked with merchandise one couldn't buy anywhere else, like Tangee nail polish and Evening in Paris perfume in its trademark opaque, blue glass bottle with the silver lid. Sunny and her friends had spent hours "shopping" this store, spending their baby-sitting money.

The soda fountain in the back looked the same, too. Sunny's mouth salivated in anticipation of the fountain cherry Coke that Ty ordered for her.

"For here or to go?" the soda jerk inquired.

"Here." "To go." They answered in unison. Ty took off his hat and sunglasses and looked down at her. "If you take it outside the ice will melt. We'll drink them here."

Sunny sat down on the stool he indicated and took off her own glasses. "You enjoy ordering people around, don't you, Sheriff?"

"I like calling the shots, yeah."

"Lord, spare me from male domination."

The soda jerk slid two icy glasses in front of them and went back to his hotrod magazine. After taking a few sips of his drink through the straw, Ty asked, "Do I detect a trace of bitterness in your prayer?"

"More than a trace."

He swiveled around on his stool to face her. "What got you so turned off of men?"

"Generally or specifically?" she asked sweetly.

"Let's start with generalities."

"Generally men want to keep women 'in their place.' "

"Hmm, I might take issue with that, at least until we determine exactly what that place is. Let's get specific."

"Specifically," she said, drawing out the word, "my application for a business loan at the bank will be considered using a different scale of standards than it would be if I wore trousers instead of pantyhose."

He looked down at her slim legs, but, sensitive to her mood, refrained from making any comment. "They turned you down, huh?"

"Not yet, but as good as."

"What do you want the loan for?"

Sunny looked at him, wondering what possible interest it was to him. None. Maybe that's why she was tempted to tell him about her plans. It might be refreshing to get the opinion of someone who would look at the matter from a purely objective standpoint, someone who didn't harbor any preconceived notions about her or her work.

"I want to go into business for myself," she told him curtly.

"What kind of business?" He finished his drink and set it aside, devoting all his attention to her.

"I design and make Mardi Gras costumes."

He stared at her for a moment. Then, to her astonishment and supreme irritation, he started laughing. Sunny snatched up her purse and sunglasses and slid off the stool. He caught her arm.

"Wait. Don't go off in a huff. I'm laughing at George, not you."

"George?"

"He told me you were a seamstress. I couldn't quite picture you bent over a sewing machine in a sweatshop."

She resumed her seat. "Well, I've spent many hours bent over a sewing machine, but I mainly do the designs, then work side by side with the seamstresses who make the actual garments. They sew, I construct."

"It sounds to me as though you're already in business for yourself."

"No, I work for a mom-and-pop company that's been in the business for years. It's a highly specialized field. I want to branch out on my own."

"Why?" He set his elbow on the pink Formica lunch counter and propped his chin in his hand, giving every impression that he was genuinely interested.

"My creativity is stymied. The couple I work for are tired. Their ideas are tired. Their lack of energy shows up in their work. The innovative designs we've produced in the last couple of years were mine. But I'm only getting paid a salary."

"That would tend to reduce your incentive."

"It only reduces my incentive to remain with

them. I have too many ideas that are begging to be made into realities. When I leave, I'll get many of their disappointed regular clients, and more clients through word of mouth. I'm confident that it wouldn't take long at all for me to become well established."

"But in the meantime you need operating capital."

"Exactly. For the million and one necessary expenditures associated with starting any business. Mainly, I'd have to make some sample costumes. Hopefully I could sell them later, but in the meantime, they would prove my talent to customers who don't know my capabilities."

Ty smiled at her lack of humility, but Sunny was too caught up in her subject to notice.

"The ball costumes are elaborate," she continued. "The materials alone for one gown cost thousands of dollars. I can't make them for nothing."

"Let me see if I understand," he said. "You submit an idea, or several, to a client. She chooses the design she wants and you make the costume for her."

She congratulated him on being so astute. "I wish you were a bank officer. I couldn't seem to pound that concept into Mr. Smithie's head."

"Bankers see only the bottom line."

"I'd only need a handful of orders this first year to show a profit. Not many new businesses can promise to do that. And I know in here," she said, pressing a closed fist against her heart, "that my costumes would be so stupendous that the year after that I'd have more orders than I could fill."

He stared down into her earnest face. "You've convinced me." Their stare held for a long moment. "Ready?" he asked at last, nodding down at her empty glass.

"Yes," she murmured, pulling things back into focus. "Thank you."

He paid their bill. "Which aisle should we take? Toys and books or feminine hygiene?"

Sunny, actually grateful to him for relieving the tension that had unexpectedly sprung up between them, shot him a sour look and started down the aisle stocked with sand pails and Rambo dolls.

"I have one question for you," he said. "What does all that have to do with making bad sketches of insects?"

"I should have known better than to believe you were taking me seriously."

"I was." He sounded offended.

"Maybe. Still, where business and the female sex are concerned, you're no different from the bankers. When you look at a woman all you see is a pair of—" She bit off the last word, castigating herself for her carelessness.

"Oh, I noticed your pair, all right. But, lovely as they are, that doesn't mean I don't see more than them."

Sunny didn't know if it had actually gotten hotter outside or if his reference to her breasts only made it seem that way. As soon as she stepped onto the sidewalk, she turned in the direction of her car. He was a constant source of irritation, but, giving credit where credit was due, he had been a good listener. She thanked him for it, then added, "I needed to vent my frustration."

"Keep your chin up," he told her, lighlty cuffing her on the chin. "Mr. Smithie might surprise you and say yes."

"It would be more of a shock than a surprise."

"If I were the bank I'd lend you the money."

"Because you believe in what I want to do?"

"Because a woman who could summon up the courage to walk out on a church full of people on her wedding day can do anything she sets her mind to."

Her footsteps faltered. "I wish you'd forget about that. But then why should you be the only forgetful one?"

Stopping, he brought her to a halt and turned her to face him. "Uh-oh. I think I found a raw nerve." He studied her bleak expression. "Smithie didn't use that as the reason for turning you down, did he?" Choosing not to answer him, Sunny continued on her way.

"That sonofabitch," she heard the sheriff mutter.

When they reached her car, she unlocked it and tried to open the door. Ty, putting his weight behind his straight arm, prevented that. She turned around, finding herself wedged between him and the car door. As evidenced by his smile, he was trying to lighten her mood.

"About that bug."

"I told you that it was a dragonfly."

"I stand corrected." His eyebrow was still arched inquiringly.

"I had this idea," she said resignedly, "of a dragonfly. I can see a black sequin casing from the top of the head to the bottom of an oh-so-tight skirt." Her forehead puckered. "I just can't figure out how I'd handle the wings. They should be enormous. Sheer, iridescent. They'd need to move to get the right effect and be strong enough to stand out away from the body. They'd have to fold up somehow, or come off completely, after she made her grand entrance."

Suddenly realizing where she was, Sunny self-consciously glanced up at Ty. He would think she was nuttier than he already did. Or be bored by her meandering thoughts. But his smile was an indication of just how much he was enjoying himself.

"Sounds good to me," he said.

"Thanks."

"Could I interest you in lunch?"

"I don't eat lunch."

"Sex?"

It was too bold a suggestion not to laugh at. "No, thank you."

"An afternoon skinny dip in the lake?"

"Aren't you on duty?"

"All right then, an evening skinny dip by moonlight." He moved closer. "Come to think of it, that sounds even better."

"Night swimming invariably leads to a summer cold."

"Sunny," he growled, "what I have in mind for us would set the lake to boiling."

His intensity made her doubt that he was merely teasing. Against her will, she couldn't help but wonder what a moonlight swim might entail. Before her imagination could carry her away, she said briskly, "Apparently you've failed to get the message, Mr. Beaumont. I'm not interested in a . . . sexual encounter with you. I'm only going to be here for a week."

"And that's the very deadline that's cramping my style."

"For winning your bet with George?"

She got only a slow, lazy smile for answer. "Consider this your good deed for the week. Help me out."

"Take a sex maniac to lunch."

He laughed at her droll humor. "I guarantee that you'll have fun. I want to win the wager. Don't make it so hard."

She searched his face, wondering if his choice of words had a double meaning, but decided it was safer not to pursue it. "I'm making it not only hard, Mr. Beaumont, but impossible."

He reached out and tracked the row of buttons down the front of her dress. He poked her lightly where they stopped, a good two inches below her navel. "Nothing's impossible."

He swung open her car door. Once she was safely inside he closed it. Then, giving her an I'll-have-you-naked-yet smile, he turned and sauntered off down the sidewalk.

Five

"Damn you, Sunny!"

The curse startled her. She raised her eyes and looked at Fran in surprise in the mirror. "What for?"

"For looking like that." Fran flung her hand toward the image in the mirror. They were in a bedroom of Fran's house. Sunny, hopefully for the last time, was trying on the bridesmaid's dress she was going to wear at Fran's wedding. "No one will be looking at me if you're standing beside me."

"Don't be silly."

"I should have my head examined for choosing that peachy-gold color for your dress." Fran sat down on the edge of the bed. "Remember those hot, fresh peach sundaes we used to make? That's what you look like."

"Peaches and cream?" Sunny laughed scoffingly. "Come on, Fran. You can do better than that cliché."

"Cliché or not, you look gorgeous. The dress is perfect, dammit. Please take it off."

Sunny unzipped the silk confection and slid it down her hips, stepping out of it carefully.

"On second thought," Fran groaned, "put it back on. The sight of your model's body reminds me that I've had two kids and several hot peach sundaes too many."

Sunny rehung the dress on its padded hanger and replaced it in a plastic bag. She shimmied out of the slip that had been designed to go under the sheer bodice of the bridesmaid's dress and, standing unself-consciously in panties only, reached for the casual slacks and top she had worn in to this fitting at Fran's house.

"You're sounding melancholy today. Prenuptial jitters?"

"I suppose."

When she was dressed, Sunny sat down on the bed beside her friend and took her hand. "What's wrong, Fran?"

Fran smiled ruefully. "I'm not fooling myself, Sunny. The five years I was married to Ernie took their toll on me, not only emotionally but physically." Tears filled her eyes. "I'm a saggy, pudgy mess. What if Steve doesn't like me?"

"Oh, Fran!" Sunny clasped her friend in a fierce hug. "You're being ridiculous. Steve loves you."

"I know he does." Fran, looking sheepish, disengaged them. "We've slept together. I wanted to make sure about that the second time. Ernie's beautiful body was all for show. He was lousy in bed." She traced the seam of the bedspread with her fingernail. "But when Steve and I were together, it was darkly romantic. I made certain he didn't see too much. But I'm worried about when we're living together, when all the lights are on and he sees just how shapeless my breasts are and how lumpy with cellulite—"

"I can't believe this!" Sunny took Fran's shoulders between her hands. "You've never had a poor self-image. Why now?" Sunny looked at her friend shrewdly. "That's not really it, is it?"

"You know me too well," Fran grumbled.

"Spill it."

"Maybe I'm having second thoughts."

"About Steve?" Sunny asked quietly.

"No. I'm crazy about Steve. But I'm having second thoughts about getting into another marriage. In a way I envy you. You've dated tons of men. I never really dated anybody but Ernie. He was the only man I could see. Then Steve came along soon after my divorce. Maybe I should have moved away for a while. Gone to the city. Exposed myself to a different life-style. Lived like a swinging single."

"It's not all it's cracked up to be, Fran. One can get very lonely."

Fran's attention immediately shifted from herself to Sunny. "Do you wish you had stayed here and married Don?"

"No, I've never regretted my decision not to marry him."

"Sunny—"

"Don't ask me, Frannie," Sunny interrupted quickly, squeezing Fran's hand as though to choke off her words. "If I ever told anybody my reason for walking out, I'd tell you. You know that." She glanced down at their clasped hands, not really seeing them. Instead she was seeing again the shocked expressions on her parents' faces when she had turned away from the altar and faced them with her astonishing announcement.

"It was something I had to do. I know people thought I was being characteristically fickle, but it wasn't like that at all. It wasn't a decision I made lightly. I would never have put my parents through something that embarrassing unless I had had a very good reason and felt that it was the wisest choice, if not the easiest. Please believe me."

"You don't have to justify yourself to me, Sunny. I'd never bring it up, except that I think *you* need to talk about it."

"I can't, Fran. Maybe sometime. But not right now."

"Okay. Anyway, it's lunchtime, and I promised the girls burgers at the Dairy Mart. Want to come along?"

Sunny smacked her lips as she jumped off the bed. "You bet. I haven't had a Dairy Mart burger in over three years."

"I wonder if they could make a hot peach sundae."

"What happened to all those grim references to sagging and cellulite?"

Fran called for her daughters, who were skateboarding outside, to get into the car. "The crisis had passed. Blame my self-pity on biorhythms or hypoglycemia or just being a nervous bride. Steve's crazy about me. Everything about me. For all the glamour in your life, Sunny, I wouldn't trade places with you for anything in the world."

Sunny wondered if Fran had discerned that things weren't always as rosy as they seemed.

"Yum-my."

"Um-huh." Sunny was enraptured by her thick, juicy cheeseburger. It was the old-fashioned, preassembly-line kind made with meat cooked over charcoal and buns grilled in butter. The French fries were fat and hot out of the grease.

"I wasn't talking about the food. I was talking about that."

Sunny glanced up from her cheeseburger basket and followed Fran's gaze through the windshield of her car. The sheriff of Latham Parish was walking toward the window where patrons of the drive-in restaurant placed their orders. Sunny could barely force down the bite, which, up until then, she had been chewing with sybaritic pleasure.

She hadn't seen Ty since Monday. All day yesterday, she thought he might phone or come by on one pretext or another. He could have used her "intruder" as an excuse to check on her. Or he might have reissued the invitation for a moonlight swim. But when he hadn't made any attempt to contact her, Sunny had vacillated between relief and vague disappointment.

"He's okay," she said offhandedly.

Fran swung her head around to gape at her. "*Okay?* Is there something wrong with your eyesight?"

They both looked back at Ty. He pushed his straw cowboy hat off his forehead and bent down to speak to the flustered girl in the window. She could barely compose herself long enough to write down his order. His bent posture showed off one of his best features, especially to the women who were sitting in the car behind him. His physique did wonders for an ordinary pair of blue jeans. Seemingly in no hurry, he was exercising his dazzling smile on the simpering waitress while waiting for his order to be cooked.

"I thought you were madly in love with Steve." Sunny's tone was peevish, though, if asked, she couldn't have specified why she was annoyed.

"I am. But I'm not blind," Fran replied. "Steve'll benefit from my sexual fantasies. *Cosmo* says they're healthy and harmless."

"And you think Beaumont is fantasy material?" Sunny was curious about him, but didn't want to come right out and ask leading questions. Perhaps Fran would take the bait and divulge information Sunny wanted.

"Don't you?"

She shrugged. "He's probably a lot like Ernie. It's all exterior packaging."

"Not the way I hear it."

"Really?" Sunny asked innocently.

"Hmm. A friend of mine told me—" She suddenly broke off, casting a quick glance over her shoulder. "Hey, girls, if you're finished, you can get out and play on your skateboards."

Her daughters, who had gulped their lunch and were restlessly waiting in the back seat for Fran and Sunny to finish, whooped with glee and, taking their skateboards with them, scrambled from the car.

"Be careful," Fran called.

At the sound of her voice, Ty turned, spotted her and waved. She waved back. He smacked the girls on their bottoms as they ran past him and warned them to be careful on their skateboards. He then turned back to the window to take up his conversation with the waitress. Because of his sunglasses, Sunny couldn't tell if he had noticed her sitting in Fran's car.

"What did this friend of yours say?" She hoped she sounded casual enough.

"Well," Fran said, stuffing a catsup-drenched French fry into her mouth, "what it amounted to was that"—she licked salt from her fingers—"he was the best she'd ever had." She swallowed her bite.

Sunny, who had nothing in her mouth, swallowed equally as hard. Unaware of her friend's discomfort, Fran drew on her chocolate malt.

"He set hearts all over town aflutter when he arrived. They haven't stilled yet."

"Where'd he come from?"

"Florida, I think. Very hush-hush circumstances. There's never been mention of a Mrs. Beaumont. Widows and divorcees have tried their best to remedy that. They flock to him." Fran laughed. "I doubt he's cooked more than three dinners for himself since he moved to town."

"So he's been involved with a lot of women?"

"No, that's the problem. He doesn't become involved."

"Oh," Sunny said unkindly, "one of *those*."

"Not exactly." Thoughtfully Fran stirred her malt. "My friend said that he laid his cards on the table before he ever folded his pants over the footboard of her bed. He told her upfront that he wasn't looking for a lasting relationship and not to expect one."

"But she didn't believe him."

"I guess not. After a few weeks of dinner dates and multiple orgasms, he stopped calling her. She was heartbroken." Fran paused in her story to shout out the window for one of her daughters to stop wheeling in the path of the other one.

"That's been the pattern with any woman he sees," she said when she resumed. "But from what I understand, he plays fair. He tells them at the outset that it's temporary."

"And they're still willing to risk getting hurt? He can't be all that good."

Fran shot her a naughty smile. "But it sure would be fun to find out, wouldn't it?" Sunny frowned; Fran laughed. "You know, Steve and I were worried about you the other night when we saw you dancing together. I didn't get a chance to warn you about him before you left the party. But then I figured you could handle him. You two are so much alike."

"Beaumont and me?" Sunny cried. "How?"

"You're both the love 'em and leave 'em type."

Sunny shrank back in her seat. "Oh."

They watched Ty take the carry-out sack from the waitress and tip his hat to her before pulling it down low on his brow again. His slim-hipped swagger, emphasized by the black leather gun belt, held them both spellbound as he walked toward his patrol car. Just as he reached it, one of Fran's daughters whizzed in front of him on her skateboard, followed closely by her sister.

"Uh-oh," Fran said.

Ty stopped both girls and crouched down on his haunches to lecture them about skateboard safety. They listened with respectful attention and followed contritely when he led them back to the car.

"Are we under arrest?" Fran asked him as he bent down to speak to her through the window.

"No." He flashed a thigh-melting smile. "But it would sure as hell brighten up the jail to lock you two in it."

"Let us off easy, Sheriff. Please," Fran teased.

"This time I just advised the girls to be more careful."

"I've advised them on the same thing," Fran said, giving her offspring an intimidating look over her shoulder. "Maybe they'll listen better to you."

"Ready for the wedding?"

"As ready as I'll ever be."

"Steve's chomping at the bit."

During their exchange Sunny sat as still and quiet as a field mouse when the barn cat was on the prowl. She jumped when Ty spoke her name. "How are you?"

"Fine."

"Any more intruders?"

"*Intruders?*" Fran exclaimed.

"No." Sunny turned her head and looked at the

sheriff with open hostility, which he seemed to enjoy immensely, if his grin was any indication.

"How's the dragonfly coming?"

"*Dragonfly?*" Fran's questions were beginning to sound alike.

"I'm still working on it," Sunny told Ty.

He nodded. "Let me know how it comes out. Well, I gotta be going or my cheeseburger will get cold. You girls remember what I told you," he said, glancing at Fran's daughters. "See you at the wedding."

"If everything gets done in time," Fran replied and added a short laugh.

"The wedding is still three days away. I'm positive that everything that's supposed to be accomplished will be."

Referring to his bet with George, he spoke directly to Sunny. Her cheeks grew pink. They were still warm long after he got into his patrol car and drove away.

Fran gazed at Sunny, who was wrapping up the remainder of her lunch. Thanks to Ty Beaumont, she'd lost her appetite. "Well?" Fran demanded.

Sunny cleared her throat uneasily. "Well what?"

"You failed to mention any intruders to me."

"Raccoons."

Fran continued to look at her as though waiting for enlightenment. "Raccoons?"

"It doesn't bear repeating, okay?" Sunny said testily.

"And I suppose the dragonfly is self-explanatory, too. What are they, code names or something?"

'Fran-nie."

"Okay, okay," Fran said, starting the car. "But if you find out firsthand what we've been speculating on, it's your duty as a best friend to tell me everything."

*　　*　　*

Sunny was concentrating so hard that the telephone rang several times before she cursed, threw down her pencil, and got up to answer it.

"Hello."

"Hi."

Ty Beaumont's voice lost none of its sensual punch through the telephone lines. She could swear she felt his breath in her ear. Her skin broke out in cold chills, even though it was the hottest time of the afternoon. She sank down onto the nearest chair.

"Wake up on the wrong side this morning?"

Sunny could hear the grin behind his words. "I'm sorry if I sounded cross. I was busy."

"Sorry to catch you at a busy time."

She lifted her heavy hair off her neck. "I needed to take a break anyway."

"Working on the dragonfly?"

"She's resolved. I'm working on a sea nymph now."

"A sea nymph, huh? That sounds promising."

"Yes, I think I have the very client in mind."

"That wasn't what I meant."

"I know what you meant."

He laughed easily. "Did you enjoy your lunch yesterday?"

Until you came along, she thought. "Dairy Mart cheeseburgers are almost as legendary as Woolworth's cherry Cokes."

"You and Fran have been friends for a long time, I take it."

"Since grade school."

"You must be enjoying your visit with her."

"Very much."

"Got a lot to talk about?"

"Always."

"Did you talk about me?"

His intuition was exceeded only by his ego.

"Look, Sheriff," she said impatiently, "don't you have any leads to follow up on? Any crimes to solve? I'm busy."

"Is this what the famous Sunny Chandler brush-off sounds like?"

She wouldn't even honor his question with an answer. "Was there something you wanted, Mr. Beaumont?"

"There's plenty I want from you. Should I give you an itemized list?"

"I'm hanging up now. Good—"

"I'll be there at seven."

"Where?"

"There. To pick you up."

"What for?"

"Charles Bronson."

"Pardon?"

"The drive-in. There's a Charles Bronson double feature tonight."

"No thanks, I don't like violence."

"I wouldn't think of getting violent. Not on our first date."

"On the screen," she ground out.

"Who goes to the drive-in to look at the screen?"

"Precisely. That's why I don't want to go with you."

"How come? Afraid I'll win my bet two days early?"

His audacity appalled her into speechlessness. She was left holding a buzzing receiver after he said, "Seven," and hung up before she could get out a word in reply.

Sunny wasn't sure why she was dressed, ready, and waiting for Ty at a few minutes before seven. Probably because she couldn't resist his dare and, too, because she hadn't liked his remark about the "Sunny Chandler brush-off."

He'd been listening to gossip, and, while she wanted to pretend that it didn't bother her, she had to admit that it did. She had no idea why she cared what he thought of her. But it seemed important that Ty Beaumont not consider her the fickle, heartless, femme fatale that the rest of the people in this town did.

She heard his car drive up and peeped through the shutters. Surprisingly, it wasn't the patrol car, but a silver Datsun 280Z. Fran's talk about healthy fantasies came rushing back to Sunny's mind when he pulled his tall frame from the low-slung sports car and walked toward her door. She was grateful for the opportunity to look at him without his knowing it. That way she was prepared for the snug fit of his jeans and the thin cotton shirt through which his chest hair was a beguiling, fan-shaped shadow.

She had a sound argument against fantasies being harmless, though. Even prepared as she was, her palms grew moist with tension as she pulled open the door and bravely confronted those blue eyes and white teeth.

"Hi. Ready?"

"Almost. Come in."

As soon as she closed the door behind him, he pulled her into his arms. She was so taken by surprise that she offered no resistance. His kiss was long and thorough, his tongue searching. He lifted her arms up around his neck and patted them into place there. He pressed his thumbs into her vulnerable underarms, then slid his open hands all the way down to her waist.

Slanting his mouth over hers at a more advantageous angle, he drew her body closer. On the move again, his hands paused at the sides of her breasts. The heels of his palms applied a light pressure to the fullness while his tongue had carnal knowledge of her mouth.

When he released her, she drew drafts of air into her collapsing lungs as she stared up at him. To lambaste him for taking such outrageous liberties would be tantamount to admitting that the embrace had disturbed her.

Instead she murmured, "I'll be right back." Somehow she found her way into her bedroom, though she was moving in a daze. The disheveled image reflected in her mirror snapped her out of the trance. Her eyes were fever-bright. They looked back at her with the dilated vacancy of a woman thoroughly aroused. Her lips were red and swollen and moist. She touched them. They still throbbed.

And her hair!

She had spent half an hour arranging it into that "casual" topknot. It was now hanging loose around her shoulders. He had taken it down without her even knowing it!

Irritated with herself, she hastily reapplied her lip gloss and picked up a perfume atomizer. On second thought, she slammed it back down on the dresser. Then, averring that it made no difference if she doused herself in perfume, absolutely nothing was going to happen in that Datsun at the drive-in, she used the fragrance liberally, even defiantly misting it between her breasts.

"All set?" he asked politely as she reentered the living room.

"Yes."

As he opened the door for her, he held out his hand. Her hairpins were lying in his palm. He didn't say anything. He didn't have to. His complacent smile spoke volumes.

"I thought you'd be driving the patrol car," Sunny remarked once they were under way.

"I'm off tonight. George is in charge of the office unless there's an emergency."

"Would you mind rolling the windows up?"

"Yes. I like the wind."

Sunny didn't doubt that. It was doing him a big favor by keeping her blouse plastered to the front of her body. The shape of her breasts was detailed for him in profile every time he turned his head to look at her, which was frequently.

She lapsed into stony silence. If he wouldn't think her a coward, she would demand that he take her home. As it was, she was resigned to spending several hours in verbal skirmishes. Those she could handle adroitly. What she wasn't sure she could withstand was his assault on her senses.

He made something sexual of shifting the car's gears. His powerful muscles moved with unconscious precision, contracting and relaxing with hypnotic suppleness. The car responded to him like a well-tamed animal. A mere flick of his wrist, a fluid motion of his leg, and it performed.

"The drive-in is on the other side of town," Sunny said, tearing her eyes away from his lap as he downshifted.

"We've got to stop at my place first."

"What for?"

His smile would have embarrassed a tomcat. "I never go to the drive-in unprepared."

She stared at him with dismay, then disgust, before turning her head away. She kept her gaze steadfastly on the windshield until they pulled into the driveway of a small, but well-kept, house on a tree-shaded street. It wasn't the kind of place she expected him to live in.

It was a family neighborhood. Children were playing on the wide lawns. Several boys on bicycles waved to Ty as they rode past. Two women were chatting over a row of dwarf crepe myrtles in full bloom. The man across the street was mowing his St. Augustine grass.

Ty came around and opened her door. "Come on in."

"I'll wait here."

"Have you got something to hide?"

"Yes."

"What?"

"Myself."

"Staying hunkered down in the car will only increase their curiosity."

He was right. By now most of his neighbors had noticed that their sheriff wasn't alone. They paused in their various pastimes to stare unabashedly. Sunny shoved open the car door. Declining to take the hand Ty offered to assist her, she alighted by herself. She also shook off the hand he placed on her elbow to help her as they took the wide brick steps up to the porch where he swung open the front door of his house.

The living room was bright and airy. Sunny had expected something dim and iniquitous. It wasn't spotless, but it was neat, as though clutter had been shoved off the modern furniture in expectation of her visit. His dust rag hadn't been as thorough as it could have been. His plants needed watering.

But it was a pleasant room that looked well lived in and hospitable, a room where books were read as often as the television was watched. Sunny would have felt comfortable stepping out of her shoes as she crossed the hardwood floors. The room inspired that kind of hominess.

"This is nice."

"Thanks," he said. "Want to see the bedroom?"

"No."

"Designer sheets. I changed them today."

"I'll pass."

"Then let's go in the kitchen."

"The *kitchen*?"

"That's where I keep them."

Sunny was too stunned not to follow him into the room that overlooked a deep backyard. Ty went to a pantry and pulled the door open. He reached inside. When he withdrew his hands, Sunny closed her eyes, not believing that he could be so . . . crude.

"Popcorn and Cokes." Her eyes popped open. He was juggling a plastic sack of popcorn and a six-pack of Cokes.

"*Popcorn and Cokes!*"

"I never go to the drive-in without them."

She wanted to scream at him. "I thought—"

"What?"

"Nothing." Her lips clamped shut.

"What did you think I came back here for?" His blue eyes narrowed on her. "Why, Miss Sunny, you can't mean—you thought . . . ? When I said I always went to the drive-in prepared, surely you didn't think I was referring to . . . I'm downright ashamed of you."

"Will you stop that nonsense? Just hurry up so I can get out of here."

Chuckling, he started to pop the popcorn. He turned on the burner beneath a pan and poured cooking oil into it, then tore open the package of popcorn with his teeth and shook the kernels into the oil.

"Make yourself useful and watch this while I ice down the drinks," he told her. "And don't let it burn. I hate it burned."

Sunny, wearing a rebellious expression, moved to the stove. Ty had placed the lid over the pan. Kernels were already exploding against it. "Doesn't the drive-in still have the concession stand?"

"Sure does," he replied as he noisily emptied ice trays into a small, portable cooler.

"Then why are we popping our own popcorn?" She shook the pan, determined not to let it scorch after his superior admonition.

"I don't consider it real popcorn unless it's popped like this. My mother used to make it this way, before automatic poppers."

"Where are your parents?"

"Neither of them is still living."

"Oh. Brothers and sisters?"

"None. You like butter, don't you?" he asked, abruptly changing the subject.

She nodded absently. "I think this is done. What should I pour it in?"

He produced a large plastic bowl with a tight lid. Since the drinks were ready, he took over the corn popping and popped two more batches before dropping half a stick of real butter into the hot pan. It hissed and sizzled and filled the kitchen with its milky aroma.

"Your domesticity surprises me," Sunny remarked, watching him as he whirled the melting butter around in the bottom of the hot pan.

"In all honesty, popcorn is the only domestic thing I do really well." His eyes moved from his task to her face. "In the kitchen, that is."

Sunny dodged his piercing stare. "Fran said that you don't eat too many dinners at home."

"So you *did* talk about me."

"I didn't ask," she said waspishly. "Fran volunteered the information."

"I see. What all did Fran say?"

"That you are a real bastard where women are concerned."

He wasn't the least bit insulted. In fact, he laughed. "That doesn't sound like something Fran would say."

"You're right. I drew that conclusion myself."

"So, you and Fran discussed my love life."

"I wouldn't call it *love* life."

"Oh?"

"I don't consider sleeping around love."

"What do you consider love? Jilting a poor schmuck at the altar?"

Sunny reacted as though he had struck her. For a moment she didn't move, but only stared at him. When she did move, it was with a swish of cotton skirt and a swirl of golden hair that almost slapped him in the face as it came around.

"Wait! Sunny!" She didn't stop. She didn't slow down. In fact, she speeded up. He blocked her path by stepping around her and bracing himself against the doorjamb. "That was unforgivably rude."

"Damn right it was. Now get out of my way."

"I'm sorry. Truly. And you're absolutely right, sometimes I am a bastard. It comes from practice."

"You admit that you are?"

"No, I admit that I *was*. Brusque. Rude. Insensitive. I've changed in the few years I've been here, but sometimes I have a relapse." He laid his hands on her shoulders. "I didn't mean to say that to you. It just came out."

"You don't owe me anything, Mr. Beaumont. Not even courtesy. I'm not one of your lovesick ladies."

His mouth twitched with the need to smile. "Fran did some fancy talking, I see."

"Apparently so do you. It gets you into a lot of bedrooms."

The teasing glint faded from his eyes. "I'm not a monk, and I require more than the clinical detachment of a prostitute, so, yes, I've cultivated sleeping arrangements with a few women in town. But I'm always honest. I've never taken advantage of a woman by making promises I know I won't keep."

Sunny lowered her head. So Fran had said. He let a woman know beforehand exactly what she was getting into. Staring straight into that muscled wall of chest with its blanket of fuzzy gold hair, Sunny could understand why some of his women went so willingly to the emotional slaughterhouse.

He placed a finger beneath her chin and lifted her head. "I haven't broken tradition yet. You knew from the beginning, moments after I met you, what I wanted."

"To win your bet."

"To get you in bed."

"One and the same."

"Hardly," he rasped. "Much as I like sipping Wild Turkey, sweetheart, I'd rather be tasting you."

Her insides took an elevator ride. "I said no," she said tremulously. "Didn't that change your mind?"

He took half a step closer. "Touch me and see."

At his bold invitation, she sucked in her breath sharply and turned her back on him. "Do you eat salt on your popcorn?"

He followed her into the kitchen. "Sure," he answered, lazily drawing the word out.

The man's moods were chameleonlike. Sunny wished she could recover from their sexual bantering as rapidly and with as much skill as he.

He took a metal saltshaker—the ugly, industrial kind with a handle—down from the pantry and shook it over the bowl of popcorn. Then he dribbled the melted butter over it.

Sunny watched the golden, liquid butter trickle through the fluffy white kernels. She decided that the only thing that smelled better than freshly popped popcorn and melted butter was Ty Beaumont. His cologne was potent enough to attract her, but elusive enough to tantalize instead of overwhelm.

He wiped the last drop of melted butter from the rim of the pan before setting it aside. Lifting his coated finger to her lips, he painted them with the butter until they were slippery and shiny.

Apparently all his neighbors had gone inside. No longer were sounds of activity coming from beyond the doors of his house. The sun had slipped far enough below the horizon to bathe the kitchen with its vermilion afterglow. The atmosphere was warm and still and silent. He emanated heat. His fingertip was smooth and firm as it unhurriedly smoothed the butter over her lips.

Sunny's heart was pounding so hard it frightened her. Perhaps that was why she spoke his name with such an imploring, puzzled inflection. "Ty?"

"Hmm?"

His open mouth moved down to hers. He barely touched her lips, only exchanged breath, until he felt her yearning body strain up against his. He flicked his tongue over her buttery lips, making low, hungry sounds deep in his throat. Licking, tasting, his tongue was nimble and wet and suggestive. Her lips parted and reached for his. Her breath came in rapid little puffs.

When she thought she might lose her mind from suppressed longing, his tongue finally breached her lips and flirted with the tip of hers. Then, making a savage sound, he pressed his lips firmly against hers. They were slick, and the slip-sliding friction was breathtakingly sexy.

"You know I still want you," he growled, keeping his lips against hers. "Don't you?" She whimpered an answer that was unsatisfactory to him. "Don't you?"

"Yes," she said, and moaned. She couldn't very well deny it when the rigid evidence of his want was rammed against her softness with a swift, masculine thrust. Mindless of the consequences, she cuddled it between her thighs and, coming up on tiptoes, rode it gently.

Ty cursed scandalously into her mouth, before filling it with his tongue. His large hands spread wide over her back and pulled her so close that her breasts were flattened against his hammering heart.

Beyond thought of anything else—his obscure past, hers—Sunny threaded her fingers up through his dark blond hair and held his head fast while the fires in her belly spread to every part of her body and threatened to consume her.

"Sunny, Sunny." Groaning, he buried his face in her neck. "It's time, isn't it?"

Her body slumped against his in surrender. When he set her away from him, propping her against the countertop, her eyes could barely focus on the face that had disturbed her dreams and been at the root of shameless, countless fantasies in the last few days.

"We'd better be going then," he said. "If we don't leave now, we won't get a good spot at the drive-in."

Six

The Gator Drive-In was packed to capacity even though it was a weeknight. Ty was heartily greeted when he stopped at the admission gate. Apparently he came to the drive-in often, and Sunny couldn't help but wonder with whom. Raising his hips, he angled his body straight beneath the steering wheel in order to fish several bills from the pocket of his tight jeans.

Since leaving his house, Sunny had maintained a stony silence. Her pouting was childish, but she was so furious she knew her voice would crack if she tried to speak.

How many times was she going to fall for his sexual sabotage? Every time he took her in his arms, she behaved out of character. Her mind became as traitorous as her body. All he had to do was touch her and her brain shut down operations. Common sense deserted her. She became as obedient as a puppet, responding only to its master's hand.

Was she getting soft? Losing sight of the grim facts of life? Men had no consciences. Hadn't she found that out the hard way? They weren't to be trusted. So why was she so compliant to the sheriff when his foreplay led to nothing but frustration?

Everyone else in town seemed to like and respect him, however. As he drove up and down the curved aisles of the outdoor theater, Ty Beaumont was honked at and waved to. He called back hellos, addressing people by name.

"There aren't any spaces left this close to the screen," Sunny commented cantankerously. He'd driven down the same rows several times.

"I know. I'm just letting all the rowdy boys know I'm here. They'll behave better."

Darkness had fallen and the credits were already rolling on the first of the double feature before he finally pulled the Datsun into a vacant space in the back row. He adjusted the speaker in the window. "Can you hear all right?" he asked.

"Fine."

"Good. I'll be right back. Stay here."

He squeezed her knee before he opened his door and slid out. The affectionate gesture startled her so much that she had a delayed reaction to his desertion.

"Wait," she cried out to his retreating back, "where are you going?"

"I'll be back."

She watched him weave his way through the rows of parked cars until he disappeared, muttering deprecations toward a man who would abandon his date at the drive-in. He returned in under ten minutes, but by that time, Sunny was stewing. "Where did you go?"

"I had to check on something."

"I hope it was important," she said snidely.

"I think so. There was a lot of dope in the junior high school last spring. I wanted to make sure the cigarette I saw those kids passing around was tobacco."

Sunny felt very small. She asked, "Was it?"

"If it hadn't been I'd be taking them to jail right now."

"Junior high kids?"

"I took an oath to uphold the law. Drugs are against the law; I don't care who's using them."

This was a side of Ty Beaumont Sunny had never seen. Gone was the teasing gleam in his blue eyes. The insinuating smile had thinned into an indomitable frown, a clear indication that he took some things, particularly his job, seriously. Ty Beaumont could be uncompromising. The thought was unsettling.

"But it wasn't pot, so we can relax." He smiled across at her, his earlier mood returning. "Ready for some popcorn?"

Sunny's mouth was dry and her stomach was jumpy, but she nodded and answered yes. For a while, they watched the movie, but neither was interested in the plot that revolved around grisly murders. Sunny couldn't keep her eyes on the screen and off the man who intrigued her in spite of herself. Every time she surreptitiously glanced at him, he was watching her. His stare made her nervous.

So much so that when he spoke to her, she nearly jumped out of her skin. "What?"

"I asked how you're surviving the week in your hometown."

"Okay. I dreaded coming back, but my visit hasn't been too bad. Only three more days and I can leave."

"Seen many people?"

She shook her head and dusted her lap free of the salt that had shaken off the popcorn. "Only Frannie and the kids. I keep to myself as much as possible. Of course you did the gossips a world of good by parading me through the drive-in tonight."

His white grin shone even in the darkness. "I've got a reputation to uphold. And so do you."

She looked away and took several sips of the Coke he had opened for her. His cold drink can was tucked between his thighs against his solid maleness. She tried to keep her eyes away from the spot.

"Heard from the bank?"

She made a sound of regret. "Not yet." A thousand times that day, she had willed the telephone to ring, but it hadn't. The deadline she had extended Mr. Smithie was fast approaching.

"No news is good news."

"That's as banal as the movie script," she told Ty.

"But I mean well. I'm only trying to make you feel better."

"I don't want to feel better," she said irritably. "I want the loan. It makes me furious to think of Mr. Smithie and his ilk sorting through my personal accounts, discussing me, judging my character on the basis of one day out of my life. What does that have to do with my ability to repay a loan? What does one have to do with the other? But you can bet when they analyze my application, that's what will be on their petty little minds."

She paused to draw a deep breath and, without knowing that she did it, turned more toward Ty and raised one knee, hooking her foot behind the other leg.

"Do they remember that I was president of the student council for three straight years? No. That I was graduated from Latham High School with honors? No. That I was on the dean's list each semester I was at LSU? No. They've forgotten all that. All they remember about Sunny Chandler is her wedding day."

"Well, you gotta admit that it *was* rather memorable."

She glanced up and caught his wide smile. "Forget it." Angrily, she put both feet on the floorboard again and faced forward. "I can't imagine why I'm talking about my business with you. You're laughing at me."

"I was smiling," he exclaimed, clearly affronted. "You know what your problem is? You're too high-strung. Always on the defensive."

"I am not!"

"See?" He pointed his index finger at her. "That's what I'm talking about. No wonder you went through the local boys like quicksilver. I'd bet that if one so much as disagreed with you on the price of eggs, you dumped the poor sucker. He was out because he didn't cater to you, pay you homage."

"That's not true."

"Isn't it? You can't stand being topped." His hand shot out and grabbed a handful of her hair. Using it, he pulled her across the console of the Datsun until her face was directly beneath his. "Let me tell you something, Sunny Chandler. When I top you, you're gonna love it."

"Let me go."

"And I'll tell you something else." Pushing the words through his bared teeth, he wound another inch of her hair around his fist. "If I'd been Don Jenkins, you would have never made it through the door of that church. Do you think I'd have let you walk out on me without so much as how-dee-do? No way. I wouldn't have let you go without a fight, and I think there's something seriously wrong with Jenkins for letting a firecracker like you get away."

"You don't know what you're talking about."

"Oh, yes, I do. I know your type. Fiercely independent. Always has to have the upper hand. The last word. You look like sugar, but you're pure starch. You keep a fellow's balls in a vise." He laughed at her shocked expression. "Well, you've met your match, sweetheart, and there's gonna be hell to pay. Beware."

Sunny, pushing against his chest, tried to work herself free. "While we're on the subject of types, I know all about yours, too," she lashed out. "You think you're God's gift to women."

"I've had very few complaints," he said arrogantly. "Certainly no returns."

"Whenever you flash that come-hither smile, you think a woman should lie down and put out and feel honored for having been granted the privilege."

Grinning in his most ingratiating way, Ty finally released her. She moved back to her side of the car. "You can sure get down and get dirty when your hackles are raised, can't you, Miss Sunny?"

Shooting him a fulminating look, Sunny rubbed the sore spot on her scalp where he'd had a grip on her hair. He was a barbarian . . . but a barbarian with insight. She did keep men at a distance. But it was to protect herself, not to tease them. In that respect Ty was wrong about her.

In a strange way, his sudden attack had excited her. No man had ever been so *physical* with her. She had liked feeling his breath strike her face on each deliberate word. His voice was laced with so much suggestion it seemed tangible. The hint of latent violence that lay just below his easygoing surface held an appeal for her that she was ashamed of.

But, as before, she refused to let him see her shaken. Instead, she pretended to be annoyed. "You made me miss a crucial part of the movie."

"You enjoy seeing cops get blown away?"

"If this kind of movie bothers you, why did you bring me here?"

"This kind of movie doesn't bother me. Hollywood could never portray it as bad as it really is."

Again, she got a glimpse of his serious side. "Were you a cop before you came to Latham Green?"

"Yes."

"In an urban area?" Sunny glanced at the screen where a high-speed chase down a city thoroughfare resulted in yet another violent death.

Ty, his eyes also on the screen, only nodded in answer.

"Why did you leave?" she asked.

He swiveled his head around and impaled her with a cold, blue stare. "Because I could no longer tell the good guys from the bad ones."

Sunny realized that she was sticking her neck out when it would have been much safer not to. Fran had hinted that Ty Beaumont's past was shrouded in mystery, but it wasn't merely curiosity that prompted her to ask, "What happened?"

"It's a long, boring story."

"I wouldn't be bored."

"I would."

"Don't you miss city life?"

"Nope."

"Not at all?"

"Not at all."

"You'll never go back?"

"Never."

As though to close the subject, he snapped the lid over their bowl of popcorn and set it behind his seat. After he had placed the cooler back there as well, he turned sideways and stared at Sunny.

"What's the matter?" she asked self-consciously.

"Nothing I can see from here. I'd say you were just about perfect."

He reached for the first button on her blouse and undid it. Moving the fabric aside, he ran his index finger over the smooth curve of her breast. The gesture took her so by surprise that it was several moments before she reacted.

"Leave it," he said sternly when she lifted her hand to do the button up. "I like looking at you." His gaze fastened on the mound of flesh that he had provocatively exposed. "It makes my mouth water."

Sunny went very still. She couldn't explain why she was allowing him to touch her this way. Maybe it was because the expression on his face was so intense. There wasn't a woman alive who could resist that kind of absolute concentration from a man.

He touched the lace trim. "What's this called?"

"A camisole."

He slipped his hand into her blouse and cupped her silk-covered breast only long enough to verify that the camisole was the only underclothing she was wearing. His hand was large, strong, warm, and Sunny was pierced to the core with desire. She wanted her breast to continue filling his palm forever. But he withdrew his hand and only smoothed his fingers back and forth across the sloping curve.

"You wear this camisole instead of a bra?"

"Sometimes."

"I like it."

"Thank you."

She wouldn't have thought an absurd conversation like this was possible between a modern man and woman. If it hadn't been for the constant motion of his stroking fingers, she would have thought she was imagining this.

"Whenever I was on a stakeout," he said reflectively, "or something really hellish had happened, I often fantasized about a woman's breast."

"Most men do."

"In a lecherous way. And sometimes my fantasies were strictly sexual, too. But often I daydreamed about breasts in a . . . I don't know . . . a nurturing sense. Sometimes in my fantasies I was peeling down a garment of lacy lingerie, like this camisole, and revealing a beautiful breast. I'd kiss it. Then lay my head there." His mouth quirked in a derisive smile. "Freud would have had a field day with me."

Sunny's throat was so congested she could hardly speak. When she did, her voice was husky with emotion and arousal. "I can understand that. The breast represented peace to you. A haven. Much like a man's shoulder would to a woman. When I feel alone, my favorite fantasy is to be sitting on a man's lap with his strong arms around me, my head resting on his shoulder. It really has nothing to do with sex."

His fingers became still, barely hovering over her skin. He lifted his gaze to Sunny's eyes. "Doesn't it?"

Mesmerized, she stared back at him. "I don't know."

For ponderous moments they stared at each other.

Ty was the one who eventually broke the silence. "What color is your camisole? It's so dark I can't tell."

"Pale pink."

"Pink." He repeated the word and smiled as though he found that delightful.

His stroking fingers were barely touching her, but Sunny was feeling the caress everywhere. Her body was purring like a well-tuned motor and was just as warm and ready to accelerate. She struggled to keep herself from moaning aloud and succeeded. But there was one response she couldn't hide from him.

He unfastened another button on her blouse and gazed down at her. He smiled. "I haven't even touched them. My voice alone did that." He fanned his fingertips over the pointed crests of her breasts. "Hmm, nice."

Desire was trilling through Sunny like the high notes from a flute. "We're missing the movie."

"We were the only ones watching it anyway. Everybody else is way ahead of us."

"But they're kids, and we're adults."

"Yeah, and you know what they say about consenting adults."

He curved his hand around the back of her neck and drew her close for his kiss. Her lips were pliant beneath his. His ardor sparked hers, and the spontaneous combustion was explosive. Sunny melted against him, crooking her arm around his neck, loving the feel of his hair against the inside of her elbow.

Ty ducked his head and nuzzled her cleavage. "You put perfume here tonight."

"Yes."

"Wonderful."

He kissed the upper swell of her breast. Sweetly. Sunny held her breath. She clasped his head tightly, burying her fingers in his thick hair, wanting to feel his warm, damp mouth on the raised center of her breast.

Instead he took it between his fingers, pinching it lightly, raising it even more, rubbing the very, very tip of it with the pad of his thumb.

"I want to kiss you right here." Sunny moaned at his erotic words. "I bet the lace would feel scratchy against my tongue." Her head fell back in a silent plea that he put action to words. "I want to make you wet." Through her skirt, he squeezed a handful of her thigh.

Shocked but thrilled, Sunny stared into his face.

Her hands were now on his shoulders. She felt the tremors chasing each other through his body. They matched her own. Speechlessly, she nodded.

Issuing a deep groan, Ty buried his face in the hollow of her throat. "I'm so hard I hurt. I've been hard since the first time I saw you eating that chocolate-covered strawberry."

With a sudden movement that bordered on being ferocious, he raised his head again and cupped her face between his palms. Alternating his thumbs, he rubbed them across her dewy lips. "Your mouth is delectable. I was fascinated by it when I saw your lips closing around that strawberry. And I wanted you to be . . ." He shook his head as though to clear it and laughed dryly. "What I wanted you to do, I would have to arrest you for. It's still illegal around here." Her stunned expression won a naughty grin from him. "For now we'll put that marvelous mouth to use doing something else."

He lowered his head to kiss her again. But they were interrupted.

"Sheriff Beaumont? Uh, Sheriff? 'Xcuse me, sir."

Ty whipped his head around toward the driver's window, where someone was pecking on the glass. The man flinched and backed away from Ty's fierce, Viking glare.

"I, uh, I hate to bother you like this, Sheriff."

"I'm off duty, Wade."

"I know that, sir, and I hate like hell to bother you, what with your lady and all . . ." He dipped his head so he could see Sunny. "A thousand pardons, ma'am."

Sunny, who had hastily and clumsily rebuttoned her blouse, was grateful that the darkness hid her tousled hair, her flaming cheeks, and her wrinkled skirt.

"What do you need, Wade?"

"Well, sir, it's sorta an emergency, I guess. If it wasn't, swear to God, I wouldn't bother you."

"Get to the point," Ty barked in a harsh, businesslike manner.

"It's Sally, Sheriff. She, uh, well, she . . ."

"What?"

"She's in labor."

"*Labor!*" Ty and Sunny chorused.

"Uh-huh, sir. When I got in from work she told me that she'd been feelin' poorly all day. I figured a picture show might perk her up some. So we—"

Ty was already in motion. He reached beneath his seat and produced a magnetized, battery-operated, rotating red light, which he set on the roof of his car. Reaching around Wade, he replaced the drive-in's speaker on its post and said to the young man, "Meet me at the exit gate. I'll escort you to the hospital."

"I sure would be obliged. Sorry again for—"

"Get moving!" Ty bellowed.

Wade tipped his bill cap and loped off. Ty, muttering curses, started his car and drove it to the exit. His impatience was hilarious. Sunny held back her laughter as long as she could. He glowered at her when he heard the first giggle.

"That hick. Doesn't even know when his wife is in labor," he mumbled.

"Isn't he one of the Florys?"

"Yeah."

"Intelligence has never been that family's strong suit," Sunny said, laughing in earnest now.

"I think they've married their cousins too many times. Hang on. Here they come." A dilapidated pickup rumbled up behind the Datsun. "Hope that damn thing can make it to the hospital."

Ty roared out onto the highway, red light flashing. He had had a siren built into the Datsun just for emergencies like this. He turned it on now and the sound nearly blasted Sunny out of the car. The wind whipped her hair around her face, and she was still laughing so hard that tears filled her eyes.

Every now and then she glanced over her shoulder. Miraculously the pickup stayed right behind them. Traffic moved aside as they sped past.

But by the time they reached the hospital and braked outside the emergency room entrance, the pickup was wheezing. White smoke billowed from beneath the hood.

Ty shoved open his door and got out. He ran toward the passenger side of the pickup, jerked open the door, and assisted the heavily expectant mother out. Her husband didn't seem to be at all in the rush that Ty was. Wade got out of the pickup's cab and ambled around the hood, scratching his head as it belched smoke.

"What do you reckon's wrong with my truck?"

Ty shouted, "Get your wife inside before she has her baby out here on the asphalt! I'll take care of the damn truck."

His drill sergeant's command galvanized Wade into action. He escorted his wife through the wide glass doors. "Thanks, Sheriff," he called back just as the doors closed behind them.

Ty climbed into the steaming pickup and backed it into a parking space. He then rejoined Sunny in the Datsun. "I just left the keys in the ignition. Who'd want to steal it?"

He replaced the portable police light beneath the car seat and made certain the siren was switched off before he engaged the gears and drove out of the hospital's parking lot.

"Well," Sunny said with an impish smile, "that was certainly exciting!"

Ty scowled at her. Then the absurdity of the episode struck him, and his mouth fashioned a wide grin. Soon the car was filled with their laughter.

"I wanted to murder him for interrupting—"

"I thought he'd never get to the point and—"

"Then when he told me—"

"I couldn't believe he hem-hawed around like that!"

Ty wiped mirthful tears from the corners of his eyes. "God, I'm starving. The excitement made me hungry. How about you?"

Without waiting for her consent, he pulled into the Busy Bee Café on Main Street, which was the only restaurant in town that stayed open late. "I haven't been here in years," Sunny remarked as he held the door open for her.

"I'm sure it hasn't changed. It's probably been that long since they've swept the floor."

Indeed the café hadn't changed, Sunny observed as they went in. The acrid smell of overused frying grease was pungently familiar. The waitress she remembered from her youth was still on duty. She recognized Sunny instantly. "Hiya, Sunny. Welcome back. Gee, you're lookin' great."

"Thank you. How are you?"

"Same as ever. Old and ugly."

Sunny slid into the maroon vinyl booth Ty indicated and picked a menu out of the metal rack on the table while Ty gave the waitress their order for two coffees. "Is that all right?"

"Perfect," Sunny said.

"I didn't even think to ask if you'd rather go back to the drive-in."

She shook her head. "I'd had enough gore to last me for a while."

"Speaking of gore, dust off the menu and let me know what you want to eat."

When the waitress brought their coffee, they both ordered a steak sandwich. "She seemed to know just how you like it," Sunny said as the waitress moved away. "You must come here often."

"On slow nights, yes."

"When you haven't been invited out."

"When I haven't been invited *in*."

Recalling their conversation about his sex life earlier in the evening, Sunny wanted to appear vexed, but found that his smile was too disarming to resist. She returned it.

The lettuce in their unimaginative salads wasn't too limp and was redeemed by the thick, creamy, homemade dressing. The sandwiches were garnished with fresh garden tomatoes. The breading on the batter-dipped and fried cutlet was golden brown and crunchy.

"Dessert?" Ty asked, as Sunny moved her empty plate aside.

"No, thank you."

She did, however, let the waitress refill her mug with hot, fragrant coffee. As soon as she cleared their dishes away, the waitress went back to watch the television set on the counter. The Johnny Carson Show was on, and the cook joined her in watching it. Ty and Sunny were the only diners in the café.

She sat staring into her steaming coffee, running her finger idly around the chipped rim of the mug.

"Where do you think we'd be if Wade Flory hadn't interrupted us?" Ty asked.

She lifted her head quickly, but when her gaze clashed with his, she lowered it again. He didn't seem to know the meaning of the word subtle. He never led up to anything gradually, but pounded home his point with the force of a pile driver. She was never prepared for his brazen statements and outrageous questions. She stalled in giving him an answer now. "What do you mean?"

"You know damn good and well what I mean. What would our hot and heavy necking have led to?"

"How should I know?"

He leaned across the table and whispered confidentially. "You know, Sunny. We'd be in bed."

Knowing that he was probably right only made her angrier. "Is that all you ever think about?"

"Not all of the time," he said evenly, "but lately, yes. I've got a wager riding on this, remember?"

She blew out a deep breath of exasperation. "If you'll leave me alone, I'll buy you a case of whiskey myself."

Wrinkling his brow, he pretended to seriously consider her offer, then shook his head. "No, it just wouldn't be the same. No challenge involved. And I'd have to buy George a new fly-casting rod."

"George! I could strangle him. He used to be so nice. I can't believe he would be involved in—" Her eyes became slits of suspicion. "Or did you just make this up?"

His smile was noncommittal.

"Did you?" she hissed across the table. "There really *is* no bet! That's only a new approach your sick mind invented, isn't it?"

Again, all she got by way of answer was a sly smile.

She scooted to the edge of the booth. "Take me home."

His eyes moved down her body. "Gladly."

"And when I get there, I'm going in alone."

"Sunny, Sunny," he said in a wheedling way, "no more petting tonight?"

"No."

"That's not fair. I hadn't even gotten my hand up your skirt yet. I'll bet half the guys at the drive-in had at least gotten that far."

He was pouting so adorably that she laughed,

her anger of a moment ago being dissolved by his charm. "You're incorrigible."

The bell over the entry to the café jangled when the door was opened. Sunny glanced in that direction. At that instant, her smile collapsed and her peachy complexion paled to the color of cold ashes.

The man who came in looked around. His gaze fell on her. He appeared to be as shocked at seeing her as she was at seeing him.

Ty, instantly aware of the change in Sunny, turned around. Don Jenkins was walking toward them.

"Hello, Sunny."

"Hello, Don."

Sunny thought that her heart was going to claw its way out of her chest. She knew, in the most literal sense, what heartache felt like. But she had to put on a brave and blasé front. The smile she painted on was too bright and too wide to be genuine, but she hoped he wouldn't notice.

"You look great," Don said.

"Thanks. So do you."

Actually he didn't. He looked haggard. Thin and stoop-shouldered. Fran's words about a marriage on the rocks came back to her, and Sunny took a perverse pleasure in the evident signs of his stress and unhappiness.

But his face was so poignantly familiar that it was difficult for her to pinpoint what was different about him and easy to savor all that was familiar, from the way he parted his hair to the habitual way he slipped his hands into his trouser pockets.

"Evening, Ty," Don said, remembering his manners. He glanced down at the sheriff, who smiled at him blandly.

"Don."

Don addressed Sunny again. "I guess you're in town for Fran's wedding."

The obvious reply was heard by all, but spoken by none. It was a wedding that had caused her to leave and a wedding that had brought her back.

"I'm so happy for her. Steve seems like a wonderful person," she said enthusiastically.

"Yeah, he's a great guy." Don shifted his weight from one foot to another. "How are things going for you in New Orleans?"

Sunny didn't have to ask how he knew where she was living. Gossip had surely leaked back to him. "Oh, I absolutely love it. I have an apartment off St. Charles near Tulane."

Impressed, he raised his eyebrows. "Nice neighborhood."

"I adore it. It's so exciting in the city. There's always something going on."

"Around Mardi Gras time, I saw your picture in the paper with one of the float costumes you had designed."

She tilted her head back. "Were you suitably impressed?"

"Yes, I was," he answered seriously.

Sunny didn't want to ask the next question, but it was pressing against the back to her throat, demanding to be voiced. "How's Gretchen?"

He rolled his shoulders once, quickly, in the facsimile of a shrug. "She's, uh, she's okay."

Their eyes met and held for several beats before Sunny said, "Well, we were just on our way out. Ready, Ty? It was so good to see you again, Don. Tell Gretchen hello for me."

Don moved out of the way so she could slide from the booth. Ty tossed a handful of bills on the table, spoke a gruff good-night to Don, and then followed Sunny outside.

She could barely wait until he opened her car

door. When he did, she all but fell into her seat before her knees buckled beneath her. Taking the lake road out of town, Ty drove just within the speed limit. Sunny rested her head against the back of the seat and let the humid wind pound against her. Not a single word passed between them during the entire trip.

Ty braked the Datsun in front of the cabin. Sunny wanted to escape without any ado. "Thanks for the evening, Ty. It was fun."

She was out of the car in a flash and running up the steps of the porch. She fumbled with her keys at the door, cursing her clumsiness when she dropped them.

It seemed that making a hasty getaway was out of the question anyway. Ty elbowed her aside, picked up the keys, and unlocked the door himself. He didn't wait for her to step inside, but pushed her in ahead of himself and switched on the light. By the time Sunny's eyes had become accustomed to the sudden brightness, he had a grip on both her shoulders.

"Let me go! What's the matter with you?" she demanded, trying to squirm out of his hold.

"That's my line, Sunny. What's wrong with *you*?"

"Nothing!"

"Then why did you act that way in front of Jenkins?"

"What way?"

He shook her slightly. "Don't play dumb. Start talking."

"About what?"

"I want to know why you walked out on your wedding."

Seven

She abruptly ceased struggling. "What makes you think I'd tell *you?*"

His face moved down very near to hers. "Because whether you want to admit it or not, Sunny, there's something going on here."

"Going on?"

"Between us."

She laughed scoffingly. "Your wager. If there is one."

"More than that."

"That's the extent of it."

"Hardly," he said softly. "Ever since I took you in my arms to dance, we've been short-circuiting. You might not want to admit it. You might not like it. But you sure as hell can't deny it."

The stubborn jut of her chin said otherwise. "Why won't you just leave me alone?"

"Because, dammit, I want you. In bed."

His bluntness gave her pause, but not for long. "You're never at a loss for words, are you?"

"Never. And neither are you, except when the topic of your wedding comes around. Then you clam up. Why?"

"None of your business."

"Yes, it is."

"By what right?"

He suddenly grabbed her hand and yanked it forward, pressing it against the fly of his jeans. "*That* gives me the right. As your next lover I have a right to know what's going on inside your head."

She pulled her hand away and rubbed the palm of it as though it had been burned. He turned her stunned silence to his advantage. "Why did you put on that stupid, Southern-belle act when Jenkins came in?"

"What Southern-belle act?"

"Sweetheart, you could have given Vivien Leigh a run for her money."

"I don't know what you're talking about."

"Then I'll be more specific. The fluttering eyelashes. The simpering smile. Your ridiculous vocabulary. 'I adore it.' " He made an impatient gesture. "Where did all that crap come from? Is that kind of posturing what Jenkins expects from you? No wonder your relationship with him fell apart."

His words stung. But rather than take issue with a point she was afraid she might lose, she attacked from a different angle. "Relationship! That's a funny word coming from you. What do you know about relationships? From what I hear the relationships you have with the opposite sex rarely last for more than one night, if that long."

"We're talking about you, not me."

"*You* are talking about me."

"It was your wedding that went bust."

"Well, at least I got that close," she shouted.

"I got closer," he shouted right back. "I got married."

For an instant, he froze. Then he turned quickly, giving Sunny his back. She watched him drive impatient fingers through his hair as he swore beneath his breath.

Sunny's chest seemed to cave in on her. "You're married?"

"Divorced."

"When?"

"A long time ago."

"What happened?"

"I got shot."

"Shot?" She sank down onto the arm of the sofa.

Slowly, he turned to face her again. He stared down at her for a long, quiet moment, then started talking in choppy phrases. "We got married. I got promoted to Vice. I loved it. She hated it. We quarreled every time I left the house. She didn't understand why—"

He stopped abruptly, raked his hair again, then resumed. "One night they called her from the hospital. The gunshot wasn't much. The bullet went straight through me." Absently, he touched his side. "But it was enough to scare hell out of her. When I recovered, she told me she couldn't take it anymore, that she couldn't live with me knowing that every time I left it could be for the last time. We divorced."

Sunny studied the striped pattern of the sofa. "Is that why you came here?"

"No. That was something else." His lips hardened into that thin line of bitterness that was becoming familiar to Sunny. It was there each time his motivation for moving to Latham Green was mentioned.

He moved to the window, opened the shutter, and stared out into the blackness surrounding the cabin. He seemed lost in morose reflection. Sunny wondered, with an unacknowledged pang of jealousy, if he was still in love with the woman who had left him. She surprised herself even more than him when she asked the question out loud.

His head came around slowly and he looked at her hard. Then a faint smile relieved his lips of their tension. "No, Sunny. If I was, I would never have let her go."

"But you look so sad when you talk about it."

"I only regret being a postponement to her happiness. I wish I had realized sooner that we weren't right for each other, that we wanted different things." He returned to where she was sitting on the arm of the sofa and crouched down in front of her. Paternally, he covered her hands with his. "Is that what happened to you and Jenkins? Did you just decide at the last minute that you wanted different things?"

"That was basically it, yes."

"What was it *specifically*? Did you want to go on breaking hearts?"

She shoved him aside and surged to her feet. "Why do you, why does everyone, assume that it was *my* fault?"

She realized too late what a telling statement that was and only hoped that Ty didn't catch it. Of course, that was asking too much from a policeman. He was trained to catch discrepancies, revealing nuances. He caught her by the shoulders and spun her around.

"Are you saying it was Jenkins's idea?"

"I'm not saying anything."

"Not intentionally, but incriminating confessions usually pop out accidentally. What happened, Sunny? What did Jenkins do?"

She stubbornly pressed her lips together. Ty studied her face, probing her turbulent eyes.

"Now that I think on it," he said musingly, "your behavior tonight in the café was odd in more ways than one. You walked out on him in that church. Therefore, seeing him for the first time since then, shouldn't you have acted ashamed? Contrite? Embarrassed?

"Instead, you tried real hard to sell him on how happy you are in New Orleans. You're not cruel. If it was truly *you* who had jilted *him,* you wouldn't have been so bubbly, rubbing his nose in how wonderful your life is without him."

She turned her head away. He pinched her chin between his thumb and index finger and snapped it back around. "Don't," she said.

"That's it, isn't it? Jenkins said or did something before the wedding that forced you to take drastic measures. Something untenable. Intolerable."

"Over a hundred people saw me turn and leave. You've heard how fickle I was," she said, flinging her head back and swishing her hair. "I changed my mind, that's all."

"Uh-uh. I can't buy that, Sunny. Something changed your mind for you. But what? What could he have done that was so terrible, so dastardly—" He stopped, staring at her incisively. "Another woman," he said softly.

Sunny wrested herself free. She began roaming the room as though looking for an avenue of escape. Her arms were crossed over her stomach. Feeling chilled to the bone, she rubbed her upper arms with her hands. She went out onto the porch, seeking warmth. The sultry air embraced her. The shadows were dense; she wanted to draw them around her for protection.

But there was no escaping the intuitive man who was unraveling the secret that no one else had guessed. He moved up behind her.

"What happened, Sunny?" No longer malicious, his voice was as gentle and confidence-inspiring as a priest's.

He had uncovered her deepest secret. She should be furious, but found to her surprise that she was almost grateful. For three years she had kept the pain bottled up inside her. It was a relief to uncork that bottle and let it all spill out.

"I had bought gold chain bracelets for all my bridesmaids. The one I had given Gretchen—" Behind her, Ty cursed. Sunny didn't stop to comment on his reaction to the name. Now that she had started, she was eager to get it all out. "—had a faulty clasp, so I had taken it back to the jeweler to be replaced."

She shivered. He laid his hands on her shoulders and drew her back against him. "The morning of the wedding, I got up early. I had a million and one things to do and wanted to get as many chores as possible done early. Delivering Gretchen's bracelet was one errand I could get out of the way. I drove over to her house. I called out when I let myself in the front door. Obviously she was still sleeping. So I crept into her bedroom."

She paused, drew a deep breath. "And found Don in bed with her."

She said it now with the same degree of bewilderment that she had felt that morning when she saw the man she would marry in a few hours, naked, in the sleeping embrace of a woman she had considered her good friend. Rage wasn't what she had initially felt. Not even anger. But profound puzzlement.

What in the world was Don doing in Gretchen's bed?

Of course the answer was obvious.

"They woke up. You can imagine . . ." Her voice trailed off; her head dropped forward; her eyes slammed shut; she rubbed the center of her forehead. "It was terribly awkward for all of us. I cursed them to perdition, then ran out."

"Did he come after you?"

"Oh, yes. He caught up with me and demanded that we talk. I couldn't believe it was happening. It was so bizarre, so unexpected. I was dazed."

"What did he say?"

She sighed and made a shrugging motion. "That it had been one of those things that just happened. He had no excuse, no explanation for it. Gretchen meant nothing to him. He loved me, was *in love* with me, wanted to marry me. He hated himself for what he'd done." Again, she sighed. "That kind of thing."

"And you believed him?"

"Yes. I guess so. I don't know."

"Had he and Gretchen been together before?"

"He swore that they hadn't been, but it didn't really matter, did it? They had still betrayed me. Gretchen telephoned in tears, begging my forgiveness."

"So you decided to go through with the wedding."

"I didn't think I had a choice. My parents had spent so much money on it. Practically everybody in town would be there. I was so confused, and there was no one I could talk to about it because I didn't want anyone to know. It wasn't as if I had weeks or even days to make up my mind. I had to decide in a matter of hours what I was going to do.

"Don kept telling me that I was being unreasonable to even consider calling off the wedding, that in the scheme of things one night out of our lifetime didn't matter. He said I wasn't taking a very modern approach, and that if I really loved him, I'd forgive him. And I thought I loved him. It seemed impossible to back out."

She fell silent. When she picked up her story, her voice sounded far away, as though she were reliving it. "It seemed impossible until the minis-

ter asked if I would commit my life to Don. And in
that instant, I knew I couldn't. If he could take
another woman to bed on the eve of our wedding,
chances were very good he'd do it again. The least
a married couple should expect from each other is
fidelity, isn't it?" She drew a ragged breath. "So
when the minister posed the question, I knew
that no matter what humiliation it cost me, I
couldn't go through with the wedding."

For a long while Sunny stared into the darkness, lost in her memories. When she returned to
the present, she realized that Ty Beaumont was
supporting her and holding her close. His chin
was resting on the top of her head. She could feel
his breath sifting through her hair. His fingers
were stroking the sides of her neck.

Suddenly the staggering consequences of what
she had just done registered with her. Ty had
tricked her into telling him what she had kept
private all this time. Not even her parents knew
why she had left the church that day. Ty's knowing invested him with power over her. Her secret
was certainly safe with Don and Gretchen. But
now, Ty knew. At best, he pitied her. His pity
wasn't to be borne!

She spun around and faced him belligerently.
Tears of mortification filled her eyes. "There! Satisfied? Is that what you wanted to hear?"

"I had no idea it would be anything so painful."

"Then you shouldn't have badgered me into telling you."

"No, we're both better off for your telling me.
What I don't understand is why you've taken the
rap for what happened. Why have you let everyone
assume that Don was the injured party?"

"You'll have to figure the rest out for yourself,
Mr. Beaumont. I'm going inside."

She swept past him, but he caught her arm and drew her back. "*Why*, Sunny?"

As she gazed up at him, her eyes filled with salty tears. "Don't you know?"

The truth hit Ty Beaumont with the impact of a .45 slug. He knew what that felt like, and Sunny's words struck him just as hard. "You're still in love with the sonofabitch?"

"Good night. I'm going in."

"Wait a minute." He pulled her back again. "That's it? That's why you took the blame instead of announcing to the whole church full of people that he and Gretchen had been screwing around, which I personally think you should have done."

"I didn't ask for your advice, then or now."

"That's why, when you saw him tonight, you looked like you'd been poleaxed before you started playing Scarlett O'Hara. How can you love a creep like him?"

"I don't expect a man with your lack of sensitivity to understand."

"Want to know what I think?"

"No."

"I think you're fooling yourself into believing you still love him. He's just the only man who ever got your goat, the only one who rejected you and not the other way around."

"You're crazy."

"No, Jenkins is. For driving a spitfire like you away. Why would the dumb bastard risk losing you? I know Gretchen Jenkins. She's a good-looking lady, but she has none of your fire, your vitality."

He cocked his head to one side. "Maybe that scared Jenkins. Maybe he knew he couldn't begin to please a woman like you. On the night before your wedding, he got nervous about it and needed to be reassured of his virility. So he took another woman—not just another woman but one of your best friends—to bed in order to prove it."

"That's . . . that's ridiculous! Real men don't have to prove their masculinity!" Sunny cried.

"Exactly."

Sunny realized he had trapped her in a corner and now tried to bluff her way out. "I never threatened Don's masculinity."

"Are you sure?"

"Of course. How could I?"

"Just by being you. Smart, talented, self-confident, self-reliant you. Some men feel threatened by women like you. Apparently Don's one of them. He needed a woman who would nurse his ego, tell him how strong and wonderful he is."

"I did," Sunny said with desperation. To this day she couldn't understand why Don had gone to Gretchen's bed. What had Gretchen given him that she'd failed to provide? What need had Gretchen fulfilled that she hadn't?

Ty said, "But you are just as strong and wonderful as he is. More so. Jenkins couldn't handle it." He closed his arms around her. "I think he's a damn fool for letting you go. And I think you're a damn fool for still imagining yourself in love with him."

She tried to twist out of his embrace, but it was inescapable. He seemed to exert very little effort, but his arms were powerful. As was his lazy smile. It obliterated Don's image from her memory. The man she loved was obscured by this one, whom she hated. Ty Beaumont always pushed the right buttons, whether to arouse her sexually or to entice her into baring her soul. She didn't know how he'd managed it, or why she'd been so culpable, but it had happened and she would never forgive him for it.

Unaware of her thoughts, Ty kept up his lulling monologue. "Don Jenkins isn't a match for you,

Sunny. The marriage would have ended unhappily sooner or later anyway. By doing what you did you only spared yourself greater unhappiness."

"How dare you stand there and presume to know what would make me happy."

"I know, all right. You need a man who'll stand up to you. One who enjoys your spiciness and isn't intimidated by it. One who matches your passion. You need someone who'll make love to you, and I'm talking hard, Sunny. And often."

"And I suppose you think you fit the bill."

He moved against her suggestively. "You tell me."

"I'll tell you only one thing," she said heatedly. "I love Don."

"Prove it. Resist me. Resist this."

He backed her against a support beam of the porch's roof and branded a fiery kiss onto her lips. Vocal protests welled up inside her mouth, but they were stoppered by his demanding kiss. She tried to move her head aside, to dodge his persuasive lips, but they followed hers relentlessly.

She pushed against his shoulders with the heels of her hands, but he only leaned closer, sandwiching her between him and the smooth cypress wood.

"All this heat," he murmured against her arched neck, "and Jenkins wanted to extinguish it."

"And you don't?"

He brushed his lips back and forth across hers as he shook his head no. "Not at all, Sunny. I want to make you burn hotter. I want to be in the very heart of your fire."

She gasped, and when she did, he sent his tongue deep into her mouth. It maneuvered with limber skill. She fought the tremulousness that crept into her limbs, draining them of strength. She denied the sensations that slowly rivered through her body, as thick and hot and bubbly as warm molasses.

He unbuttoned her blouse and tugged the tail of it from the waistband of her skirt. "No," she protested weakly.

"Why not?"

"Because I hate you."

"Love isn't doing you any good," he said, moving his hands over her aching breasts. "Maybe you should try hate."

"Stop," she groaned.

"Before I've had a taste of you?"

"Yes."

"You want me to leave you alone, right?"

"Yes."

"No, you don't."

"Yes, I do."

He laid his lips against her ear and pressed his hand flat against her stomach, fingers pointing downward. "Should I stop here?"

"Yes."

"I can give you pleasure, Sunny, with just my fingertips. With just a touch."

"No. Stop."

"You don't want me to touch you where you're all warm and creamy?"

"No," she sobbed.

"You're a liar, Sunny Chandler," he whispered huskily.

Sunny wanted to collapse against him. She longed to rest her head on the welcome support of his chest and draw on his strength. And, with scalding shame, she admitted to herself that she wanted his hand caressing her until the achy, feverish longing was banished.

But she struggled against her weakness and raised her head. By an act of will she converted her passion to animosity. Her lips were bruised, marked not only by their kisses, but also by her own teeth in an effort to hold back her cries of surrender. Her golden eyes were glittering with defiance.

"All you've proved is that I'm human, made of flesh and not of stone. I'll go to bed with you now if that's what you want. You can win your wager. You can salve your phenomenal ego by maintaining your bedroom track record." She drew a shaky breath. "But when it's over, I'll still love Don. And you'll know that my heart wasn't in it. I'll have used you just as you've used me. Is that what you want?"

Ty had made a serious tactical error and he knew it.

Cursing his poor judgment, he drained the umpteenth cup of coffee he'd drunk since returning from Sunny's lake cabin. He hadn't even gone to bed, knowing that it would be useless. He wouldn't sleep. Between desire and self-flagellation, he'd stay awake all night anyway. So he had chosen to brew a pot of coffee and wait out the night with it.

Now, as the sun was creeping over the eastern horizon, he still remonstrated with himself for the way he'd bungled things last night.

When backed into a corner any wounded animal was going to scratch. When he had told Sunny she didn't, *couldn't,* love Don Jenkins, it was predictable that she would swear on a stack of Bibles she did.

Why had he realized that too late?

"Because I'm stupid, that's why," he mumbled as he left his chair. He rinsed his cup out at the sink, unplugged the coffee maker, and made his way through the shadowed house toward his bedroom. He happened to glance at his reflection in the mirror over his dresser. He had the blood-shot, bleary eyes of a drunk after a three-day binge. His beard was much darker than his hair and heavily shadowed the lower half of his face. His shirt was unbuttoned all the way, the shirttail hanging limply against his thighs. He looked thoroughly disreputable and nothing like the way the chief law enforcer of Latham Parish should look.

Lathering his face at the bathroom sink, he once again reviewed the events of last night. Sunny was all woman, no doubt about it. A sensuous, passionate woman. It had made her mad as hell for him to cut their foreplay short and rush off to the drive-in. If he had carried her from his kitchen into the bedroom, she wouldn't have resisted. Oh, she might have put up some token resistance, her nature being what it was, but no real resistance.

He had decided after their first meeting that the only way he could woo Sunny Chandler was by not doing anything. It had become immediately apparent to him she couldn't be flattered; she was inured to flattery. She couldn't be cajoled; she was too smart. He couldn't appeal to her pity; she wouldn't have believed him.

Instinctively he had known that the only way he could successfully get her into his bed was to inform her outright of what he was going to do, and then not try very hard to do it. Come on strong and then retreat. Confusion was the key. By the time he made his final move, the poor girl would be so confused by his clever tactics she would be relieved to fall into his bed.

All had been going well and according to plan. But he hadn't counted on the monumental road-block of her fancying herself still in love with Don Jenkins.

He cut himself on the chin. He cussed the dull blade and angrily tossed the disposable razor into the wastepaper basket. Shedding his clothes, he stepped into the shower and turned on the faucets full blast. Maybe the hard spray would beat some sense into his skull.

In love with Jenkins! Ha! What a crock of crap.

He soaped himself, frowning at the thought of Sunny still besotted by that wimp. Couldn't she see Jenkins was wrong for her? Didn't she realize everything he'd said about Jenkins's insecurity was true? Sure, it was armchair psychology. But it was so obvious any idiot should be able to see his theory was well founded.

Jenkins was the only man ever to hurt her. She was like a child who had been denied one single toy out of a boxful. Jenkins was the one she wanted only because she knew she couldn't have him. If she had truly loved him, as she claimed, she would have forgiven him any indiscretion and married him anyway. Why couldn't she see the truth?

Ty turned off the water and stepped out of the shower. He dried himself in a hit-or-miss fashion. Padding naked into his bedroom, he began plowing through his bureau drawers looking for underwear and matching socks.

Sunny knew how to give just as much as she got. She'd scored a major point by calling his bluff and telling him she'd go to bed with him. Just for sex. No emotion.

Why the hell hadn't he taken her up on that offer? Why hadn't he scooped her in his arms and hauled her into the bedroom? He would have pumped thoughts of Don Jenkins, and any other man she'd ever met, right out of her mind. At least he would have gotten rid of what he was now having a helluva time stuffing into his briefs.

He cursed his swollen manhood. Cursed the golden woman who had made it that way. Cursed his own susceptibility to her. Cursed himself for not going to one of the many women who would have been all too willing to make his underwear fit this morning.

Dressed now, he snatched up his car keys and left his house. His patrol car started right up, though one would have thought the engine was reluctant by the way Ty floorboarded the accelerator. Thankfully, the streets of town were just coming to life and there wasn't much traffic.

The sun was barely up, but it was already hot. His shirt was sticking to his back when he entered his offices at the courthouse. He was sporting a deep scowl and a tiny piece of toilet paper on his chin to stop the bleeding from the cut.

"Hi," George Henderson said, turning around as the door crashed closed behind Ty. "Coffee's almost ready."

"I don't want any. Did you get those reports typed up yesterday?"

George was taken aback by the abrupt question. "Yeah. They're on your desk."

"It's about time," Ty grumbled.

Ty's dark mood was uncharacteristic. So was his mussed, damp hair, which looked like it had gone uncombed since his shower. So was the aimless way he prowled the office as though looking for something to strike at.

"Bad night?" George asked guilelessly.

"What's that supposed to mean?"

"Nothing. I was just asking."

"Well, don't ask. I'll be in my office."

His hand was on the doorknob when George halted him with another brave question. "How's our bet going?"

Ty whirled around. "You haven't won it yet."

George laughed. "I haven't lost it, either, according to your mood."

Ty stalked into his office and rattled the glass

when he slammed the door. He flopped down into his creaky leather chair and planted his boots firmly on the corner of his desk. Leaning back, he closed his eyes.

Sunny's image was vividly imprinted on the inside of his eyelids. And just as vividly he remembered the way her breasts had looked behind that damn silky, lacy, crotch-grabbing temptation called a camisole.

He dug into his stinging, gritty eyelids with his fingertips and stifled a groan he was afraid his deputy might hear. Why was he torturing himself this way? Why hadn't he taken her last night and ended this thing once and for all?

Because he had known that one romp in bed wouldn't end it. His wanting her went way beyond the ridiculous wager with George. He wanted more than one night. He couldn't fathom a time in the near future when he wouldn't want her. Or in the distant future for that matter.

She wasn't like all the others he had bedded lustily but emotionlessly. When he took Sunny to bed, he wanted more than their glands to be involved. He wanted everything—emotions, fears, dreams—to play a part in their lovemaking.

But why?

Because she intrigued him. She put up a nonchalant, sophisticated front he'd seen straight through the minute he spotted her from across the room at the country club. She had a vulnerability she kept carefully concealed. He had wanted to discover the source of it. Last night he had.

So, fine. Now that he knew why she'd been so beguiling, why wasn't he content? Now that he knew Sunny Chandler's deep, dark secret, why wasn't he satisfied? He had no one to blame but himself for not taking her up on her offer to go to bed with him. What was wrong with him?

The heat. The humidity. He could blame his itchy skin and short temper, his sleeplessness and sexual arousal, his fantastic fantasies and foul mood, on the weather.

Or he could squarely face the grim alternative.

He had fallen in love.

Eight

Sunny rolled out of bed and stumbled through the cabin to answer the telephone extension in the living room. It had been almost dawn before she fell asleep, and then she hadn't slept well. Her head felt like it was stuffed with feathers, but there were bowling balls trying to push their way out through her eye sockets.

"Hello?"

"You had quite a night!"

"Hi, Fran." Yawning broadly, Sunny folded herself into one of the easy chairs and drew her feet up beneath her. "What's going on?"

"Absolutely nothing with me."

"How can you say that? You're getting married tomorrow." Sunny closed her puffy eyes. The sunlight streaming into the room through the open shutters was blinding.

"A mere wedding pales in comparison to the experiences you've been having lately."

"Like what?"

"Like going to the drive-in with Ty Beaumont. Then running into your ex-fiancé at the Busy Bee."

"I see the tom-toms have already been drumming out the news this morning," Sunny said dryly. "Don't you want to know what we ate?"

"Steak sandwiches."

"I was only kidding, for crying out loud!" Sunny exclaimed. "Who was the source of all this information?"

"I've had several calls from people who took in the Charles Bronson double feature last night. The consensus is that neither movie was as exciting as seeing you in Ty's Datsun. When Steve stopped for doughnuts at the Busy Bee this morning, he heard the rest."

"Unbelievable," Sunny muttered.

"So, how was it?"

"The movie or the steak sandwich?"

"Come on, Sunny," Fran said with aggravation. "Your date with Ty. Your first meeting with Don. Take your pick."

"One was as ghastly as the other."

"Running into Don so unexpectedly like that, I can imagine how terrible it must have been. What did he say?"

"You mean the grapevine hasn't supplied you with a word-by-word playback?"

Her snide question dampened Fran's enthusiasm. "Are you mad at me?"

Sunny massaged her throbbing forehead. "No, Fran, I'm not mad. I didn't mean to sound so bitchy. Forgive me for taking out a pounding headache and a sleepless night on you."

"Why the headache?" Fran asked sympathetically.

"Seeing Don upset me. I admit it."

"What did you say to each other?"

"Nothing really. 'How are you?' 'Fine. How are you?' That kind of nothingness. It wasn't so much what he said as how he looked. Bedraggled."

"He's always looked hangdog to me. Frankly I think he uses that self-effacement to evoke pity."

Fran's theory came so close to echoing Ty's that Sunny lashed out defensively. "I don't think his marriage with Gretchen is happy."

"I know it isn't. But everybody knows he took her on the rebound from you." When Sunny failed to respond, Fran said, "So if Don is responsible for your headache, that leaves me to assume that Ty's at fault for your sleepless night. Dare I hope that you went sleepless because you were otherwise occupied?"

"No, you dare not," Sunny said tightly.

"Does your crankiness stem from disappointment or relief?"

"Relief. Thank God I don't ever have to see him again."

"Not see him again? Sorry, my dear, but you'll see him tonight."

"I'm spending tonight with you."

"Right. After the wedding rehearsal."

"*Ty* will be at the rehearsal? Why? In what capacity?"

"Best man. Didn't you know?"

"Correct me if I'm wrong, but aren't you supposed to be smiling?"

Sunny's expression was as about as far from a smile as one could get. She marched up the aisle of the church, ignoring her escort as much as the situation allowed. Which wasn't much.

By virtue of its sheer size and strength a body like Ty's wasn't easy to ignore. He had shortened his long stride to accommodate hers, so their thighs seemed to move in perfect coordination while they maintained the measured tread in time to the swelling organ music. His cologne was so familiar to her now she smelled it in her dreams.

They reached the end of the aisle. In the church foyer, she withdrew her hand from the crook of his arm and turned to face him, having put it off for as long as she could. She had dreaded the wedding rehearsal, and it was proving to be just as difficult as she had anticipated.

Since it was a casual rehearsal, she had worn white jeans and a navy blue big shirt, the long tails of which were tied in a knot at her waist. Her hair was pulled into a ponytail.

Her tomboyish appearance had been intentional. She had wanted to curtail any romantic notions Ty might still be entertaining. However, when she had breathlessly entered the church, running late, he had looked at her with unconcealed amusement that told her he had gleaned her purpose and that it hadn't worked.

"You never mentioned you were going to be Steve's best man," Sunny accused him stonily.

"Surprised?"

"Unpleasantly so."

"What difference would it have made if you'd known?"

For one thing, she could have prepared herself for having to walk down the aisle with him at the conclusion of the service. It was going to be difficult enough to do it tomorrow, given the circumstances of her last march down the same aisle. Having Ty Beaumont at her side only compounded her anxiety over it.

"I might have resigned as maid of honor," she answered tartly.

He laughed. "But you didn't."

To avoid his mocking smile, Sunny glanced down the church's center aisle. Fran and Steve had been detained at the altar. The woman in charge was giving instructions to Fran's daughters, making certain they understood where to stand during the ceremony and on what cue to start back down the aisle.

Sunny wished they would hurry. For all practical purposes, she was alone with Ty in the hushed atmosphere of the sanctuary. Considering why he had left her cabin last night in such a wrathful temper, being alone with him was awkward.

"I couldn't resign," she said, "so all I can do now is grin and bear it."

"But you aren't grinning. We've come full circle. Isn't this where we started?"

"I don't feel much like grinning."

He leaned down and whispered, "Because we're an 'item'?"

"Yes," she shot back angrily. "And it's no wonder, the way you paraded us through the drive-in last night."

He shrugged dismissively. "Part of my job."

"You were off duty!"

Several heads at the front of the church turned in their direction and the instructions were momentarily suspended. From the back of the church, Sunny smiled weakly in apology.

Ty spoke out of the corner of his mouth. "The scene in the Busy Bee had enough drama to keep the gossips humming for the *next* three years. Do you plan to supply them with something to talk about on a regular basis?"

"Oh!" Clenching her fists at her sides, Sunny ground her teeth together. "You're—"

"Wait," he said, holding up his hands in surrender. "Before you start slinging mud, let me tell you what I went shopping for today."

"I don't give a—"

"A fly-casting rod."

She bit back her next words and stared at him in surprise. "A fly-casting rod?"

He bobbed his head in affirmation. "You know what that means, don't you?" She looked at him warily, her expression rife with mistrust. "It means I'm calling off my bet with George."

"Why?"

"Because there's no way I can win it, is there?" She raised her chin a notch. "There never was."

He rubbed the back of his neck and shook his head with chagrin. She was fond of the way his hair grew in a swirl around the cowlick on the crown of his head, but hated herself for noticing it, and hated even more her desire to touch it.

"I should have listened the first time you said no. It would have saved me a lot of, uh . . . dreams." He paused for a single heartbeat as his eyes focused on her mouth. "And it would have spared you a lot of aggravation." He smiled an all-American, good guy smile that would have warranted him a white hat in any Western movie. "We're maid of honor and best man. We can't let this hostility between us spoil Steve and Fran's wedding. So, what do you say? Are we friends?"

He stuck out his hand. Reflexively Sunny jumped. She stared down at his hand with open suspicion, then cautiously laid hers in it. They shook hands solemnly.

"Whew! That's a load off my mind," Ty said with a happy grin. "Now I can relax."

"Did somebody say something about relaxing?" Steve asked. He, Fran, and the rest of the wedding party had joined them in the vestibule. Steve was tugging at his necktie. " I could use a drink."

"You sound like a desperate man," Fran teased him.

"I am." He drew her close and nuzzled her ear. "I have to wait one more night to get in your bed. Legally and officially, that is." He said it only loud enough for her and Ty and Sunny to hear. Ty laughed.

Playfully, Fran fended off Steve's amorous attack. "Why don't you come over for sandwiches, Ty?" she asked. "Sunny will be there. She's staying with me tonight."

"Thanks. That sounds great," he agreed with a smile. Draping his arm around Sunny's shoulders he added, "Especially since my good pal Sunny will be there."

It took a full five minutes to decide who would ride in which cars on the way to Fran's house, since Ty had walked to the church from the sheriff's office and Fran's daughters wanted to ride with their grandparents. It was finally decided that Fran's father would drive Sunny's car and that the bride and groom and their attendants would all go in Steve's car.

"Oops, I forgot about those things in the back seat," Steve said when they reached his car. There was a tuxedo hanging on the hook and a shoe box on the seat, along with several unopened wedding gifts.

"No problem. We'll have room if Sunny doesn't mind sitting on my lap." Accommodatingly, Ty climbed into the back seat.

Sunny couldn't protest. The car had bucket seats, so she couldn't crowd into the front with Fran and Steve. Besides, Ty didn't give her a chance to offer an opinion one way or another. He reached through the door, grabbed her wrist, and, giving it a sharp tug, pulled her in with him.

She landed solidly in his lap. He spread his knees wide and, placing his hands on both sides of her hips, situated her against him. There followed what seemed to be an inordinate amount of movement necessary to get her bottom settled in his lap, but finally he was satisfied.

"Comfy?" His lips moved directly over her ear.

"I'm fine."

"It's a good thing we're only friends. Otherwise I might get . . . embarrassed."

Sunny stared at the back of Fran's head, sitting perfectly still and doing everything possible not to cause friction between her body and Ty's. He didn't seem to know what to do with his arms in the confines of the space they had. After trying several positions, he wrapped them around Sunny's waist. He clasped his hands together loosely, interlacing his fingers. Since the knot of her shirt-tail was in his way, he let his wrists relax, which lowered his hands into the V of her thighs.

Steve and Fran were engaged in conversation so they didn't hear when Sunny turned her head slightly and muttered, "I know what you're trying to do."

"What's that?"

She gave Ty a dirty look over her shoulder.

He laughed. "Believe me, Sunny, if I were trying to do something improper, you'd be the very first to know." She couldn't argue with that. The pressure building up beneath her hips made his statement indubitable. "So why don't you just sit back, relax, and enjoy the, ah, ride."

Relax? Oh, sure. Relax while his thumbs were nestling in the grooves at the tops of her thighs. How could she relax when her senses were spinning out of control? For the life of her she couldn't remember why it had seemed like a bad idea to get involved with him.

But is was, and later the reason would come to her. In the meantime, she had to put space between them. She wouldn't be able to breathe normally until she did. When Steve's car rolled to a halt in Fran's driveway, Sunny grappled for the door handle and all but tumbled out when the door came open.

For the next hour she was afforded that coveted breathing space. She and Fran stayed busy in the kitchen stacking sandwiches and taking drink orders while the other adults, including Ty, helped corral the little girls, who were too excited about the wedding to be well behaved.

Both Fran's parents and Steve's bade them an early good-night, knowing they would have to rest up because they were dividing the girls between them during the week of the coming honeymoon.

"I've got to get them settled down for bed," Fran said wearily, after sending the two youngsters upstairs.

"I'll help," Steve volunteered, rising from his chair at the table. "That is, if you don't mind hanging around a while longer, Ty."

"Take your time," Ty replied with a negligent wave of his hand. "I'm in no hurry."

"I'll drive you downtown as soon as the girls are asleep." Steve left the kitchen to join Fran upstairs.

"I guess cleaning up the kitchen falls to us," Sunny said brightly, after a considerable silence in which she and Ty stared at each other across the littered table. Palsy-walsy wasn't exactly the way she would describe the way he was looking at her. He might have said he wanted them to just be friends, but his smoldering expression conveyed something else entirely.

Sunny wondered how such an unromantic setting as Fran's cluttered kitchen with its loud, daisy-print wallpaper could be so redolent with sexuality. Yet the atmosphere teemed with it.

"I'll wash," she said, coming out of her chair as though ejected by a mechanical spring. At the sink she began rinsing the dishes and placing them in the dishwasher.

"Can I tell you something friend to friend?" he asked as he carried a tray of dirty dishes from the table.

"Sure."

"You've got a terrific fanny."

Sunny was bending over the dishwasher. She popped erect and spun around to face him, slinging soapy water onto the front of his shirt. "I can't believe you said that."

"You don't believe your fanny is terrific? Take my word for it."

"I mean," Sunny said impatiently, "that you call yourself a friend and yet say something so . . . so . . ."

"Sexist?"

"Yes!"

"Well, hey, I only learned how to be a friend tonight. You can't expect me to change from a woman-denigrating chauvinist to a good buddy in the space of a few hours."

"That reminds me of a saying, something about a leopard and his spots."

"It's not like I was trying to pick you up in a singles' bar," he said easily. "Then I could understand it if you objected to my saying something like, 'You've got a terrific fanny.' But I was just being honest, friend to friend."

"Well then, friend to friend, thank you."

"If you didn't want people to notice your behind, you shouldn't wear tight white jeans that cup—"

"All right! Thanks for the advice. I'll keep it in mind. Now, can we talk about something else?"

"Okay. How about your tits?"

She rounded on him, ready to do battle. Instead, when she looked into his teasing eyes, she started laughing. "That's better," he said. "I was getting worried about you."

"Why?"

"Don't take this the wrong way. You look as beautiful as always. But when you came into the church tonight, you looked tired." With the tip of his finger, he traced the violet crescent shadows beneath her eyes.

"I didn't have a very good day," she confessed.

"Or night?"

"Or night."

"Are you sorry we didn't sleep together?"

"No!" She took a step back.

"Sure about that?" he drawled. "I know my mood would have been greatly improved if we had. The atmosphere is oppressive. Barring a good, drenching rain, I think some raunchy sex would help clear the air."

"Is that your cure for everything?"

"Not for everything." He closed the distance between them. "But it sure as hell is for what's ailing me."

Fighting the magnetic pull of his eyes, Sunny turned away. "I had my mind on other things today."

"Did you see Jenkins?"

Sunny was surprised by his harsh question. "Of course not. Why should I?"

"I thought that maybe after seeing each other last night, you two might be on again."

"He's married!"

"That doesn't seem to matter these days."

"It does to me."

"According to gossip, Jenkins's marital status is subject to change," he said. "He might be free soon."

"I don't care. I still wouldn't want—"

Sunny heard her spontaneous protest, but couldn't believe she'd spoken it. Ty reacted by looming over her like a predatory animal about to pounce. His eyes zeroed in on her face. "You still wouldn't want what, Sunny?"

"Thank heavens, they're down for the night," Fran said, as she and Steve made an untimely entrance into the kitchen.

Ty and Sunny sprang apart.

"Maybe the girls will let you sleep late in the morning," Steve said, kissing Fran's forehead.

Sunny tore her gaze away from Ty's penetrating stare. Nervously she clasped her hands together in an effort to get a grip on herself. "I'll see that they do. You stay in bed, Frannie, for as long as you can. I'll fix their breakfast and try to keep them quiet."

"You're taking the word brides*maid* in the most literal sense," Fran said, smiling her gratitude.

"It's getting late," Steve said, "and Ty can't go home until I drive him back to his office for his car. So . . ." He turned to Fran, a wistful expression on his face.

"Sunny, we haven't carried your stuff in yet," Ty said suddenly. "Remember you asked me to help you with it?"

Puzzled, she stared at him. His eyebrows were sliding up and down like an elevator that had run amok. "Oh," she said, getting his drift. "Yes, I would appreciate your help, Ty. Excuse us a minute."

She slipped through the screened back door. Ty followed closely on her heels. Both were shaking with suppressed laughter. "They needed a few minutes of privacy but were too polite to ask for it. Was I subtle enough?" he asked.

"Before I caught on, I wondered what in heaven's name was the matter with your eyebrows."

When they reached her car, she opened the rear door and began transferring her belongings to his waiting hands. She had an overnight bag, the dress she was going to wear in the wedding, and a change of street clothes.

"Is that it?" he asked.

"Yes."

"You travel light."

They retraced their steps across the lawn. When they were still a distance from the house, they saw Steve and Fran through the screen door. They were in each other's arms, their mouths locked in a fervent kiss.

"Uh, maybe we ought to wait a minute before barging in." Ty stopped at the redwood picnic table and set Sunny's things on it. He sat down on the bench and guided her to sit down beside him.

The warm night closed in around them. The branches of the tree overhead were dense. From them cicadas sang their mating songs. There was just enough moon to cast wavering shadows over their faces in ever-changing patterns.

"You heard from Smithie, didn't you?" Ty asked quietly.

Sunny looked up at him. His intuition had hit the bull's-eye again. "How did you know?"

"And the news wasn't good."

Her mouth twisted with remorse. "No. The news wasn't good. Amid a lot of effusive apologies and well wishes, he turned me down."

"Damn!"

She smiled humorlessly. "I've already said as much."

"So what will you do?"

"I haven't decided." There was a vertical dent of worry between her brows. Her posture, the slight pucker of her lips, were testimonies to her dejection.

Ty propped his elbows on the table behind them and leaned back. "Why sweat it? Why put yourself through the humiliation of begging for money? Give up on the idea and consider yourself lucky that you won't be responsible for a business. It would probably have been one colossal pain in the butt anyway. You would—"

"I can't give it up," she cried angrily. "What are you talking about? Consider myself lucky," she scoffed. "I *want* to be responsible. I want—" She broke off when she noticed his wide, white smile. "You were playing devil's advocate, weren't you?"

"It worked, didn't it?"

She ducked her head shyly. "I guess I just made up my mind."

"No, your mind was made up a long time ago. You won't quit until you have succeeded. All I did was remind you of that."

"I can't give up yet, Ty, I just can't," she said fiercely. When she realized that her hand was on his thigh, squeezing it to emphasize her determination, she hastily removed it.

After a long, quiet moment, he said, "Must be nice."

"What?" Sunny raised her head to look at him, then followed his steadfast gaze to the back of the house, where Fran and Steve, still with their arms around each other and rocking slightly back and forth, were whispering together.

"Oh. Yes." Sunny was uncomfortably aware that Ty's hand was idly strumming her back.

"In a way I envy them," he said. "The love affair. The marriage."

"Yeah, it must be really tough, being the town stud."

"Is that what I am?"

"Aren't you?"

"I get my share."

"I don't doubt it for a minute."

Still looking through the screen door at the

embracing couple, Ty said musingly, "Sometimes I think it might be nice to sleep with the same woman every night. But I suppose it would eventually get boring."

"It wouldn't have to." Sunny was dismayed over his caustic attitude toward marriage.

"You don't think so?" He seemed to ponder that for several moments. "You might be right, but you'd be swapping the exciting and unique for the familiar."

"Personally I think there's something to be said for the intimacy that comes with familiarity," Sunny said defensively.

"Maybe. That ease with each other is certainly missing in brief affairs. If you were married, the getting-naked step wouldn't be so awkward. A married man could walk right up to his wife and start undressing her without either of them feeling self-conscious. In fact, if they were sexually harmonious, they'd probably get a helluva lot of pleasure just out of the undressing ritual."

"I think so."

"He could lift her hand, kiss the palm of it, then press it right against his . . ." He glanced down at her. "You know what I mean."

"Yes, I know."

"Good. I thought you did," he said, smiling. "He would show her how to caress him for maximum pleasure, because he would want her to feel how hard he could get, how badly he wanted her. He could bend down and kiss her breasts, caress them with his mouth and tongue, without having to wonder if she was going to like it. He would already know that that was one of her favorite forms of foreplay. Right?"

Sunny opened her mouth to speak, but nothing came out. She merely nodded, then managed a hoarse "Right."

A wayward strand of hair was lying on her cheek. He leaned forward and blew on it gently until it relocated and settled in front of her ear, the one with the two diamond studs in it. He seemed entranced with the way the diamonds sparkled through that wispy strand of hair.

"Yeah, I see what you mean, Sunny. Marriage has its benefits," he said. "But after a while, the same old thing night after night would no doubt get tiresome."

"I don't think so."

"Oh?" He tilted his head back to see her better.

Sunny wet her lips. "Not if they wanted to please each other."

"Hmm, and not if both of them had a spirit of adventure."

"Yes, and . . . and if they cared enough to make each other happy in and out of bed."

"That almost sounds like love, Sunny." He took her earlobe between this thumb and index finger and toyed with the two diamond earrings. "Are you talking about love?"

"I . . . I guess I am."

"Then it really wouldn't matter how they went about it, would it?" His gaze met hers. The heat rising out of them melded their gazes together. "Anything they did would be making love. When he put his body inside hers, it would be more than sex. Though, God knows, that would be great. But it would entail love and trust and commitment, things like that." Visually, he feasted on her face. "And there wouldn't be any reason for him to rush it. He could stay nestled inside her for a long, long time, as long as he liked. Even after they fell asleep lying face to face." He pressed his forehead hard against hers and squeezed his eyes shut. "Damn, Sunny, talking about it has made me want it really bad."

Sunny knew the feeling. She wanted nothing more at that moment than to be experiencing exactly the kind of intimacy Ty had painted in word pictures. She wanted to tilt her face up to his, touch his lips, take his tongue into her mouth. She even made a yearning sound and the initial movement to do so.

But he raised his head away from hers and with a rueful smile said, "But that's not for us. You're happy living independently in New Orleans. And, as you've said, I'm the town stud." He stood up. "Well, here comes Steve. G'night, Sunny. See you at the wedding."

No one could tell from Sunny's appearance just how dark and gloomy her mood was. On the outside, wearing the dress that perfectly complemented her coloring, she looked like a sunbeam. Radiant. Glowing. But within, she felt as lifeless and dull as cold metal.

When she had walked down the aisle, she had held her head up proudly, but standing through the ceremony at the altar had been pure hell. She had felt just as many stares boring into her back as there had been watching the bride and groom exchanging their vows.

She had avoided looking directly at the best man, but, like moths to a flame, her eyes seemed determined to die in the fire of his steady, blue gaze.

Then she took Ty's arm and left the church by the center aisle, she kept several inches between her body and his. Her attitude was unfriendly and stoic. They might have been strangers. Speculative stares followed them, some laced with resentment and envy. She wanted to stop and tell those women she had laid no claim to their sheriff, and they could fight over him for all she cared. She wasn't in the competition. As soon as this wedding was over she would never have to look at him again and that suited her just fine.

Only another half-hour, she thought to herself now as she surreptitiously checked her wristwatch. Fran had told her the reception would last no more than an hour. She and Steve planned to make a quick getaway because they were taking an evening flight to St. Thomas out of New Orleans.

The whole ordeal couldn't be over soon enough for Sunny, whose feet ached from the tight new pumps, almost as much as her cheeks ached from smiling insincerely. Lord, she couldn't wait to leave this town. She planned never to cross the city limit signs of Latham Green again after she escaped them this time.

Maybe she would leave tonight instead of tomorrow as she'd originally planned. Why wait? There was nothing to keep her here. If she got back to the cabin by—

"Sunny?"

Her head snapped up at the familiar voice. "Hello, Don."

She had seen him and Gretchen on the church lawn after the ceremony and several times during the reception, drifting in and out of her range of vision as they mingled with the other guests. Gretchen wouldn't meet Sunny's eyes. Sunny had felt a pang of regret over the loss of that friendship, but knew it couldn't be helped.

Don asked, "Can I talk to you for a minute?"

"We are talking."

"I mean in private." She was about to tell him no, but he rushed to say, "Please, Sunny. We owe each other that much, don't we?"

She turned and left the church parlor where the reception was being held. Don followed her. She stopped in the hallway outside. "I think this is as private as it should get," she said.

He looked nervous and kept shifting from one foot to another in a way she had once thought endearing, but which now irritated her because it made him appear indecisive.

"I've thought about calling you a lot," he began.

"I'm glad you didn't. It would have been awkward. And wrong. You're a married man, Don."

He laughed mirthlessly. "How well I know." Sunny didn't remark on his lack of enthusiasm. "It's . . . Gretchen and me, well . . . Did you know she's pregnant?"

Sunny was surprised, but not crushed. Why not? she wondered. Not long ago, the idea of Don's child growing inside Gretchen's body would have been unbearably painful. "No, I didn't. Congratulations."

"Don't congratulate me," he said with a grimace. "She shouldn't be having this baby. The marriage has gone sour and this is Gretchen's last-ditch effort to hold it together."

"You shouldn't be telling me this, Don. Excuse—"

"Sunny, please." He caught her hand when she tried to move away. "I need to talk to you."

"I don't want to hear about your marriage. It's none of my business."

"But it is. I made a big mistake, Sunny. A terrible mistake. I told you that when you caught me with . . . uh . . . the day we were supposed to get married. I guess you didn't believe me. Anyway, I forgive you for walking out and making a fool of me in front of the whole town."

She recoiled as though he'd slapped her. "I don't recall asking for your forgiveness," she hissed angrily. "Don't you dare put me on the defensive. I did nothing wrong. I covered up for you and Gretchen."

"I know, I know. Don't get mad. Please. Just hear me out."

He glanced over his shoulder as though afraid someone might see them. Sweat glistened on his forehead. Sunny made the ludicrous observation that he didn't sweat as attractively as Ty Beaumont did.

"Sunny, I still love you," Don said with desperation. "I'm not happy with Gretchen. She's . . . she's nice and all, but she's not you. And with the baby coming, I feel trapped. Yeah, that's it, I feel trapped."

To his consternation, Sunny began to laugh. "I'm sorry, Don," she said, watching the incredulity break across his face. "There's nothing funny about what you're saying. It's just that I think this is probably the same speech you gave Gretchen three years ago. On the night before your wedding to me, you suddenly felt trapped and had to do something naughty just to prove you were still free to."

She shook her head with pity for him. And for herself. For three years she had clung to the memory of a deep love that hadn't existed. He was a shell of a man. Weak. Always blaming others for his unhappiness. A whiner. Why had it taken her this long to realize it?

"I'm sorry you're unhappy, Don. Really I am."

She turned her back on him and started down the hallway. "Sunny, I love you. I never stopped loving you. Doesn't it mean anything?"

She faced him again. "All that it means, if it's true, is that you're as big a fool as I am. Goodbye, Don."

She was in no condition to stay. Tears were standing in her eyes, precariously close to overflowing. She would make her excuses to Fran later, and, being the friend she was, Fran would understand.

Sunny brushed past a small crowd of people standing in the breezeway and rushed toward her car. Seconds later, she was speeding down the lake road, the wind playing havoc with her hairdo.

She left a cloud of dust in her wake, but rising out of it like a specter was the sheriff's car. When Sunny saw it in her rearview mirror, closing in on her, she cursed. Instead of slowing down, as the flashing red lights dictated she should, she accelerated.

Nine

She drove right to the edge of the porch before stopping the car, then racing up the steps. She let herself in the front door and slammed it closed behind her, taking only a second to lock it. She ran through the large common room to her bedroom and immediately began unzipping the long zipper down her back.

She had to get the dress off. She wanted no reminders of weddings or marriage. She had to get away from everything bridal once more and forever. She had to flee this place.

"Sunny, unlock this door!"

She heard Ty's shout and the pounding of his fists on the front door, but she paid no attention. Instead she stepped out of the silk dress and flung it across the room where it settled in the corner like a landing parachute.

"I'm warning you," he shouted.

Sunny smeared her makeup as she wiped tears from her eyes. What a fool she'd been to think herself still in love with Don. All that heartache, for nothing. All that pain, for nothing. Why had she borne the humiliation and ridicule? Why had she protected him?

She kicked off the dyed-to-match pumps. Then she stood stock-still. The sound of splintering wood, accompanied by vicious cursing, was followed by heavy footfalls in the living room.

Sunny stepped through the bedroom door, disbelieving that even Ty would have the nerve to break down her door. But it was standing open, hanging by one hinge, still vibrating from the impetus that had shattered its lock. And Ty, eyes as cold as a frozen fjord, jaw set as though hewn out of stone, was crossing the living room with a stride so determined that Sunny's racing heart stalled.

At some point since leaving the church, he had shucked his black tuxedo coat and untied the bowtie. It was still hanging around his neck; that made him seem even madder somehow. The collar button of his formal shirt was undone, though the onyx studs were still in place between the pleats.

Fascinated into immobility by the fury he personified, Sunny maintained her position in the hallway. When he reached her, he jerked her up so sharply and so high that her toes dangled above the floor, barely touching it. "I ought to wring your neck for driving like that."

"Leave me alone."

He was the last person she wanted to hassle with, especially after last night, when he had once again verbally led her down the primrose path only to pull back with a casual "g'night, Sunny." She wasn't going to fall for his glib charm. Not now. Not ever again.

"Get out of my house," she shouted up at him. "How dare you break—"

"Shut up! Didn't you see me behind you?"

"Yes!"

"The flashing lights?"

"Yes!"

"Why didn't you stop?"

"I didn't want to."

"What were you trying to do, kill yourself?"

"No!"

"Are you so heartbroken over that simp that you'd kill yourself because of him?" He shook her slightly. "He's not worth it, you little idiot. Can't you see it?"

Yes, she did. Ty's harsh condemnation of her foolishness was no more severe than her own. She had wasted three years grieving over a man who had been magnified in her mind as much more than he actually was. She had been in love with an image, a figment that had risen out of the ashes of her decimated ego.

In that instant, she acknowledged the enormity of her folly and slumped against Ty. He supported her while her tears trickled inky stains down the front of his white tuxedo shirt. Then, dipping his knees, he curved one arm beneath her legs and swung her up into his arms.

He carried her into the living room and lowered himself into one of the overstuffed easy chairs. Keeping her on his lap, he wrapped his arms around her and held her close, tucking her head safely beneath his chin.

Then he did nothing but let her cry. He indulged each racking, cleansing sob. Her tears ran out before his patience did. Even then, he sat still and silent while she hiccuped against his chest.

Only when they had ceased did he use a crooked finger to tilt her chin up and her head back so he could see her face. Using his thumbs, he wiped away the muddy tracks running down her cheeks.

"Better?" Sniffing, she nodded. "He's not worth crying over, Sunny."

She blinked away lingering tears and brought him into cleaner focus. "I know."

"You know? Then—?"

"I wasn't crying over Don. I was crying for all the time I've wasted mooning over him."

His eyes, which had been moving over her face compassionately, became still. Gruffly he said, "Tell me about it."

Sunny, staring at the base of his throat where she could see a strong and steady pulse beating, began talking slowly. "For three years I've lamented what was probably the best thing that could have happened. I should have thanked Don and Gretchen. What they did prevented me from making a dreadful mistake."

Ty kept one hand resting on her thigh. With the other he went searching through her mass of hair looking for pins. One by one he removed them and watched as each heavy curl unwound and fell against her bare shoulders.

"Don needed a woman who would nurse his insecurities. I can see that now." Sunny absently moved her head around to facilitate Ty's questing fingers. "He needed a wife who would devote her life to him at the exclusion of everything else, including any personal ambitions."

Ty laid his collection of hairpins on the end table at his elbow and began combing his fingers through her hair, giving some semblance of order to the disarranged tumble of golden curls. "He needed a hausfrau who worshiped him," he said gently. His gaze moved over the sensuous woman curled up in his lap. His eyes lighted on her ankle bracelet. "You hardly fit that image."

"Nurturing him would have been a full-time job. I wouldn't have had a career beyond that."

"And what about the nurturing you need?"

"I've managed to live without it."

"Why?"

She knew he was playing devil's advocate again, forcing her to voice thoughts as they became clear to her. "Fear," she said, "of being hurt."

"Hurt?"

"Disillusioned, maybe."

He smiled tenderly. "I think so."

She returned his smile and laid her head on his shoulder. For several minutes they said nothing, only enjoyed the peace and comfort and unity of the moment.

"Ty?"

"Hmm?"

"This is the enactment of my fantasy."

Several heartbeats thrummed by before he angled his head back and looked down at her. "Had any others?"

His mouth had never been warmer or softer as it moved over hers. It had never tasted so good, and Sunny dared to let her tongue dart between his smooth lips for more.

Twilight, filtering through the shuttered windows and spilling through the door, which was still hanging open, forgotten and unimportant, cast the room in shades of lavender. Shadows were deep, but not ominous. The evening air was heavy and sweet with the summery scents of honeysuckle and magnolia and gardenia.

The only sounds made were those of nocturnal animals coming out from their daytime covers, and of night birds calling to each other through the trees, and of the lovers sighing against each other's lips when they finally drew apart, and of Sunny's stockings scratching against each other as she shifted her legs and tried to become smaller and needier within his embrace.

"Sunny, Sunny." Her name was a soft groan coming from Ty's damp lips. With her assistance, he began extracting the studs of his shirt from their holes until they were lying next to the hairpins on the end table and Sunny's hand was resting inside the starched cloth and touching the furry warmth of his chest.

As their kiss deepened, his hand curled around her throat. His fingertips stroked her neck as though in awe of its softness. Inside his shirt, Sunny's fingers were delicately exploring, tweaking clumps of crisp hair, testing the suppleness of muscle, finding and fondling his firm nipple.

He swore in a hoarse whisper and dropped his hand over her breast, cupping the fullness inside her slip. The silk shifted beneath his moving caresses, deliciously abrading her skin. Even the rustling sound it made was erotic. Her breath was nothing more than a catching noise in her throat when he lightly pinched her nipple to a peak.

"Ty?"

"What, darling?"

"Don't stop touching me this time."

"Not a chance."

She kissed his strong, tanned throat all the way down to his chest. She parted his shirt wider and pressed her lips against the solid curve of his chest where she could feel the rapid beating of his heart.

He kneaded her breast, repeatedly sliding his thumb over the hard bud at its tip, before his hand slid down to her waist, which he squeezed affectionately. Then he laid his hand on her knee. The skirt of her slip had worked its way up and was now bunched around her hips.

He raised his head from the hollow of her shoulder, where he had been planting ardent kisses, and stole a glance at her legs. They were sheathed in pale stockings. She was wearing a garter belt. Ty could see the lacy suspenders where they met the stockings at mid-thigh. The sight was so sexy it made his loins thicken with a lust so potent he wondered if he could contain it.

He slipped his hand beneath one of the suspenders and caressed her satiny thigh. A current of white-hot sensation shot through Sunny and she cried out his name. She flung her head back; her lips parted in a silent, but earnest, appeal for his kiss. He was all too glad to grant her request.

Their kiss was unashamedly carnal. As he sent his tongue in search of the back of her throat, his thumb inched up her thigh and stroked her cleft. Once. Twice. Sunny arched her back. Her hands, buried in his hair, clenched and threatened to pull out every single strand.

"Let's make love, Sunny."

She tried to nod in agreement, but her neck felt limp and useless while every other part of her body had never felt more alive. Ty came to his feet, effortlessly bearing her to the bedroom where he stood her beside the bed.

His gaze was ravenous as it moved over her, taking in her golden eyes, glassy now with passion, her moist, coral lips, and the riot of hair that shone like a halo in the fading light. Made of silk, her slip clung to the body that Ty had wanted to possess ever since he first saw it.

Her shoulders were broad, but had a feminine slope. The complexion of her throat and chest was smooth and creamy and slightly tinted from her suntan. Her breasts were high, round, taut. The nipples were standing out, enticingly, beneath the silk slip.

She reached for the thin shoulder straps and began to lower them. "No," he said, staying her hands. "Leave it on."

Before she even had a chance to wonder why he didn't want her to undress, he was drawing her against him. His kiss robbed her of all other thoughts save how much she wanted this man, filling her, ridding her of the emptiness she had lived with for so long, restoring her faith in romance, reassuring her that she was desirable.

His hands slid up the backs of her thighs. He squeezed the firm cheeks of her bottom. He held her against the stiff projection behind his trousers until their breathing was so rough and fast that kissing was no longer possible.

He pushed his hands down into the elastic waistband of her panties and rubbed his palms against her bare flesh. Sunny offered no resistance as he worked the scanty garment down her thighs and released it at her knees. She stepped out of the panties.

"Lie down."

Sunny did as he instructed and watched as he yanked off his cummerbund and let it fall. He unfastened his formal trousers and pulled them down, stepping out of shoes and pulling off socks in the process. He had more difficulty taking off his briefs, and there was no secret as to why. He was full and hard when he came to her, still wearing his unbuttoned tuxedo shirt. The black bowtie was still dangling incongruously beneath his collar.

He lay directly atop her, settling his body between her thighs as his hips nudged them apart. Cupping her head between his hands, he ravaged her mouth. When his tongue couldn't plunder it any more thoroughly than it had already done, he flicked it over her lips and used it to wash away the salty tracks of her tears.

"As of now, this second, you've forgotten Don Jenkins," he rasped. "He no longer exists for you. Understand?" For answer she arched her hips against his erection. He might have smiled, but it was difficult to tell in so intense a face. "There's only you and me now, Sunny. And I'm going to make all your misery well worthwhile."

He levered himself up and raised her slip. His eyes closed momentarily and a spasm of longing swept over his face as he gazed down at her. He knelt between her open thighs. He played with the lacy garter belt, feathered the soft tuft of fair curls beneath it, caressed the smooth belly above it.

He eased himself down over her again, this time planting his hard flesh snugly against the pouting lips of her sex. His hands smoothed over her breasts. Her beaded nipples drew his fingers like magnets. He kissed them through the slip, thrusting his tongue against the stiff crests as though he wanted to spear through the fabric.

Indeed, impatience overcame him. He tried to work the slip's strap off her shoulder. It snapped. Neither Sunny nor he paid any heed to the damage because her breast was suddenly free and her nipple was in his mouth and he was sucking it greedily while his hand massaged her upward until she surrounded his lips and chin plumply and firmly.

"Oh, God, you're wonderful," he murmured. "Someday I'll taste your milk."

Sunny gasped, first at the startling thing he'd said, then at the sudden pain of his entering her. But she clung to him tightly, lifting her hips off the bed to greet him.

"You're so small." His breath was a gentle wind in her ear.

"I'm sorry."

"I'm not."

Their mouths met in an ardent kiss as he pressed deeper. When the kiss ended, he was gazing down at her. His eyes were deeply blue and very gentle. "You're a virgin, aren't you, Sunny?"

Lying about it would be ridiculous when the proof was undeniably hindering his entrance. "Technically."

"That's the only way that counts."

"I don't know why you should be surprised," she said with asperity. "You heard the rumors that I'd never gone all the way."

He grinned. "Mind you, I'm not complaining."

"You're not?"

His eyes shone with a fierce light as he withdrew. "No."

"Then what are you . . . ? Don't stop, Ty."

"I'm not," he assured her, affectionately running his hand over her hair, her cheek. "I'm just going to make it easier for both of us."

He gave her exposed breast a fond kiss, then lightly fanned his thumb over the wet nipple while his mouth moved to her bare stomach. One deep, damp kiss after another was planted in the erotically fertile softness of her belly. He playfully nipped at the lace trim on her satin garter belt and blew against the crinkly blond down.

Then he lowered his head between her thighs. His hair tickled the supersensitive skin. He pressed his mouth against her. It was open, warm, giving.

Sunny clutched handfuls of his hair. Her head thrashed upon the pillow. Her feet were arched to a ballerina's point. She followed the groove of his spine with her toes, the gold chain around her ankle dancing along his skin.

They were unimaginable, these tidal waves of sensation that originated at the tip of his nimble tongue and rippled through her entire body to the very furthest extremity of her soul. When they gained enough impetus to engulf her, she rode them with ageless undulating motions. They came upon her as rhythmically as heat waves rose out of the ground in the summertime and were just as shimmering.

By the time she collected her scattered sensibilities, Ty was fully imbedded inside her, stretching her accommodating body. In fact, it was greedy and squeezed him higher inside her than he had anticipated going.

He grunted his pleasure. "Don't let me hurt you, sweetheart."

"You won't."

"Can you feel that?"

He moved. Sunny sucked in her breath sharply, not in pain but with renewed passion. "Yes."

"Hurt?"

"No, no."

"Feel good?"

"Yes."

"Should I do it again?"

"Yes, again. Yes, Ty, yes . . ."

"Cold? Want me to pull the sheet up?"

"No." Sunny sighed contentedly.

Lying naked in Ty's embrace was so splendid that she didn't want either of them to move for a very long time. Eternity, perhaps. He had finished undressing her with such tender care that it seemed incongruous with the hot glow of desire that was still burning in his blue eyes.

"You've got goose bumps."

"That's because that tickles."

"What? This?" He trailed his fingers down her side again, from beneath her arm to her waist. She giggled and broke out in another case of cold chills. "Sorry, but I like the side effects too much to stop."

"The side effects?" she asked. He touched the

rosy, pointed tip of her breast. Sunny moaned with pleasure. "Hmm, yes, the side effects are wonderful."

"There are marks on them. Was I too rough? Did my beard scratch?"

"Yes, and it was delicious." Her grin was that of a very naughty girl.

Ty continued to fondle her, immensely pleased that she afforded him the access to her body that he craved. She made no pretense of being modest. Their nakedness seemed to delight, not distress, her. She hadn't rushed from the bed to wash right after their lovemaking. Instead she had curled up against him like the affectionate, sensual woman he had always known she would be.

Now, propped up against the wall behind him and gazing down at her head where it rested on his stomach, Ty spread her hair out over his middle, rearranging the curls frequently, knowing that it would be impossible to discover a finer form of entertainment.

This languid aftermath to lovemaking was new to him. Even with his wife sex had always been a culmination, an ending, not a beginning. Not so with Sunny. He knew that when, eventually, they would have to leave the bed, he would do so with tremendous regret.

"Why didn't you ever sleep with Don, Sunny?"

"Is that any of your business?"

"No."

"So?"

"I'm curious."

She ran her fingers through the soft body hair that grew toward the satiny stripe which bisected his stomach. "I wanted to. He thought we should wait."

Ty's laugh was unkind and unflattering to the

other man. "I don't wonder. He was afraid he couldn't measure up."

Impishly, she touched the part of him that was now taking a well-earned rest. "I didn't know until now that the saying had a literal application."

Ty winced with pleasure, but continued with his train of thought. "He wasn't the man for you and he knew it. He didn't want you to find it out until after he had married you. You were what he wanted, but everything that attracted him to you also scared him."

She leaned her head back and looked up at him. "Am I so scary?"

"You would be to a man who's afraid to call your bluff."

She gave him a dirty look, but replaced her head in his lap. "If you're so expert on the whys and wherefores of marriage, why haven't you tried it again?"

"I never found the right woman."

"Latham Green has a limited selection. The city would have afforded you more choices."

"But I couldn't stay in the city."

She heard the change in his voice. The words were spoken with clipped emphasis. They were harshly, bitterly spoken. Sunny hated to disrupt the mellow mood, but she wanted to know what haunted him. He had helped her unlock her own emotions, to correctly label them and deal with them. Maybe she could help him in the same way.

"What happened, Ty?"

"I left."

"But why? Tell me."

She felt the muscles beneath her head contract as he wrestled with his decision. Finally his stomach muscles relaxed and he began talking.

"My partner and I, who was also my best friend, were put on this top-level case. Security was high. Very few people knew about it.

"We understood from the beginning that it was a dangerous assignment. We were to smoke out the leaders of a dope ring, who were suspected to be within the department itself."

Sunny soothingly strummed his thigh with her fingertips. He was still tense, and she knew what an effort it was for him to talk about this painful episode in his life. Yet she felt that it was a catharsis he needed.

"Our investigation went on for months. One night my partner called me at home. He was excited. A paid informer had given him some news that wouldn't keep. I agreed to meet him in a coffee shop. We were careful not to discuss anything over the phone. There was always a chance that our quarry was on to us."

He fell silent. Several moments passed. Sunny could feel his fingers moving through her hair, otherwise she might have thought he had fallen asleep; he was lying that still.

"Apparently they were," he said. "My partner hailed me from across the coffee-shop parking lot as soon as I pulled in. I went toward him." His voice cracked. "The first bullet hit him right between the eyes. Then the others, one right after the other, slamming into him—"

"Don't, Ty." Sunny turned her face into his stomach, pressing it into the hair-dappled skin. Her arms went around his waist and hugged him tight. "Don't think about it anymore. I'm sorry I asked you."

"No. I've needed to talk about it for a long time." He drew in several deep breaths. "After he was murdered, I doubled my efforts to find the bastards who were responsible." He snorted a bitter laugh. "The main culprit ended up being the head of the Vice department, the very one who had sent us out to crack the case."

Sunny made a sympathetic sound. "What happened?"

"I nailed him. He's serving time. They couldn't pin my partner's murder on him, so he got away with that. They offered me his job."

"Why didn't you take it?"

"I didn't want it. I was sick of it all. Sick of the administrators who would just as soon have slapped his hands and said 'No-no,' than have the department's corruption exposed." He heaved a sigh. "So I left and came here where I might still do some good."

"You're a man of integrity."

"Or a fool."

She looked up at him with unwavering, unqualified admiration. "A man of integrity."

"Thanks."

She kissed the pink scar in his side. "They tried to kill you, too, didn't they?"

"Yeah. The same night they shot my partner."

"And that's when your wife left you?"

"She issued me an ultimatum. If I went back on the case, she would leave me." He stroked the top of Sunny's head. "I couldn't just walk away and leave it unfinished. I had to get to the bottom of it."

"Why didn't you bring her here with you when it was all over?"

He tugged on one of Sunny's curls. "By then I realized we weren't right for each other under any circumstances." His eyes danced with teasing lights. "She wasn't as hot as you are."

She started to protest, but changed her mind

and smiled seductively. "I haven't even warmed up yet."

She lowered her lips to his stomach and dusted it with airy kisses. The smell of his skin was intoxicating and she longed to taste it. Her tongue touched him tentatively, then became so ambitious that it left the whorls of dark gold hair damp.

"Sunny," Ty ground out. His hands slid beneath her hair and loosely clasped her head. He allowed it freedom to move from spot to spot. There was only a slight tensing of his fingers against her scalp when she lowered her head to his thighs. She kissed them. Then between them. And her lips stayed until his need was desperate.

"No, Sunny," he said raggedly when she moved to straddle his lap. "I'm too hard. I'll hurt you."

Shaking her head no, she slowly lowered herself upon him.

Lying face to face with her in blissful lassitude several minutes later, Ty pushed the damp curls off her cheeks. "You shouldn't have done that," he said softly.

"You didn't like it?"

"You know better. But you could have hurt yourself."

"I was having too good a time to notice any discomfort." She kissed his lips softly. "While we're remonstrating, you shouldn't have done what you did, either."

"Putting my finger there?"

She blushed. "I went a little mad, didn't I?"

"Yes, and it was beautiful." He pondered her face as though seeing it for the first time. "*You* are beautiful, Sunny."

"Thank you."

"I don't mean it lightly. And I'm not just talking about the way you look. It should be obvious to you by now that I like the way you look very much." He traced the shape of her chin with his finger. "But I also like and admire the person you are."

Sunny's eyes misted with tears. "You do?"

"Very much," he whispered. Then he cocked his head to one side. "You're not going to cry, are you?"

"I might."

"No crying allowed in my bed. Guess I'll have to think up something to divert you."

He was extremely gifted at creating diversions.

Ten

Sunny woke up before Ty did. She came awake slowly, deliciously, with a Sunday morning languor that brought a smile to her lips even before she opened her eyes.

Slanting beams of sunlight were striping the hardwood floor. Dust motes filled the room like fairy dust. Outside, birds were chirping happily. Sunny could believe that this perfect morning was the continuation of a fantasy were it not for the man lying beside her.

He was breathing deeply and evenly. She lay there, listening to his breathing and loving the masculine, snuffling sound of it. She basked in the heat his long, hard body radiated. They were curled together like two kittens. Her cheek was resting against his ribs. His fingers were ensnared in her hair.

From now on, for every day of her life that she didn't wake up beside Ty Beaumont, she would miss this feeling of oneness.

The thought of living without him was a dismal one.

Three years ago she had thought she was dying

of a broken heart when she escaped to New Orleans. Now, she realized she had only been suffering from shattered pride. Leaving today, leaving Ty, *that* would be heartbreaking.

She loved him.

And she was angry at him over it. The arrogant, aggravating cad had made her fall in love with him.

She moved her head just enough to enable her to look into his sleeping face. In spite of herself she smiled. He was breathing through his mouth; his lips were slightly parted. Her tummy fluttered with remembrance of all the pleasure those lips were capable of giving her.

Was that all she felt for him, sexual infatuation?

She answered the question before it was completely formed in her mind. No, it wasn't just sexual attraction. She liked his sense of humor though at times, over the past week, his laughter had been at her expense. She liked his sense of fair play and his innate kindness.

He was sensitive. Last night he'd been a big brother before he'd been a lover because he had intuitively known that's what she had needed. She appreciated the confidence he showed in her skill as a businesswoman. He didn't scoff at her ideas. He wasn't condescending. He offered advice, but didn't preach.

She admired him for picking up his own life after it had fallen apart. Faced with political corruption, he hadn't turned his head and looked the other way, though the temptation to do so must have been great. Against incredible odds and without a single ally, he had withstood adversity until he had seen justice done. He was a man of integrity and high moral character. He held himself accountable for his own mistakes and didn't pass the blame to someone else. He was certainly a man worthy of love.

Between him and Don Jenkins there was no comparison.

Sunny knew that if she lay beside him much longer, she would touch him, and touching him, as she knew from experience, led to making love. She didn't want to make love right now. She needed time to sort out her feelings, to think, evaluate, plan.

Without rousing him, she slid from the bed and crossed the room on tiptoe. She dressed quickly and quietly in a pair of shorts and a loose cotton top and silently left the room. Ty was still sleeping.

Going into the bright living room, Sunny hugged herself, barely able to contain the happiness that bubbled like champagne inside her. She was in love! After years of loneliness and bitterness, she felt vitally, vibrantly alive.

But what was she going to do with this newfound love? Pack it with her other belongings and return to New Orleans? This was Sunday. Her week in Latham Green was officially over. She was free from obligation to stay.

But now, instead of looking forward to leaving, she was reluctant to. Didn't her ambiguous feelings toward Ty Beaumont warrant at least another week of testing? Surely. However, she'd made such a point about leaving on Sunday that he would wonder why she had suddenly changed her mind. And out of sheer cussedness, she wasn't about to be the first one to broach the subject of love.

Deep in thought as to what excuse she could use for staying, she wandered out to the front porch. Maybe she could say that her parents had asked her to oversee some renovations on the cabin. Or maybe—

A case of Wild Turkey was sitting on the second step.

Warm as the morning was, Sunny went cold at the sight of it. She stared down at the case of bourbon as though it were the most repulsive thing she'd ever seen. Something hideous. Foul. Too vile to look at.

That bastard!

At some imprecise moment in time, she had reached the conclusion that there had never been a bet between him and George Henderson. She had decided the wager was just Ty's clever excuse to keep pestering her until he had indeed gotten into her bed.

To discover now that there *had* been a wager, and that it *had* been taken seriously by both parties, was almost as shattering as finding Don in bed with Gretchen.

When had Ty claimed his victory? When he finally went to close the front door they had negligently left standing open? Had he crept to the telephone and placed a gloating phone call to George then? While she was lying in bed, stretching in languid sublimity over what had already happened and in anticipation of what was yet to come, had he telephoned George and heckled him about being the loser?

Her heart was tearing in two, but Sunny stubbornly refused to let her stinging tears of humiliation and disillusionment fall. Barefoot, she stamped back through the house and into the dim kitchen. She yanked drawers open, noisily rattling their utilitarian contents as she searched through them, then slamming them closed when she didn't find what she was looking for.

When she did, she stalked back out to the porch and bent over the heavy cardboard carton. Dangerously wielding the screwdriver, she pried the industrial staples out of the cardboard, then tore into the box.

The first bottle of whiskey to be hurled at the wall of the house made a racket as loud as a blast of dynamite in the quiet morning peacefulness. Glass flew everywhere. Whiskey splattered everywhere. The aroma was pungent.

Sunny, far from satisfied, didn't stop with that one. In quick succession she broke three more bottles. She was furious over being deceived again, and even angrier at her own naïveté. After shattering four bottles, she paused for breath, her chest billowing in and out from exertion and rage.

"If this is how you intend to wake me up every morning, we're off to a rocky beginning."

She spun around at the sound of his voice. Ty was leaning on the doorjamb, ankles crossed, one shoulder propped against the bare wood. He was wearing only his briefs and they rode low on his narrow hips. His hair was adorably tousled. The lower part of his face was smudged with whiskers. She could barely see his eyes because he was squinting against the bright sunlight and his brows were pulled down into a deep frown.

"You've got your nerve," she ground out, "to even show your face to me."

"How come?"

She spread her arms wide to encompass the case of whiskey and the fragrant mess she'd made. "This is all last night meant to you, isn't it?"

His scowl deepened. He shook his head with what appeared to be disgust, then said, "I'm gonna make some coffee."

A second later Sunny was staring at the gaping front door.

Her temper exploded. How dare he turn and walk away when she hadn't even begun to tell him how contemptible she thought he was! She strode into the kitchen. Ty was measuring coffee into the metal basket of the percolator. While she stood there fuming, he filled it with water, then struck a match and held it to the gas burner. Only when he was satisfied that the flame was right, did he turn and look at her inquiringly.

"Get out of my house."

"Sunny," he said on a long-suffering sigh as he leaned against the draining board and folded his arms over his naked chest, "let me give you a lesson in morning-after etiquette. The least you can do to repay a man who gave you seven orgasms—or was it eight? It's hard to tell with a woman as lusty as you—anyway, the least you can offer me in return this morning is a cup of coffee."

"You're disgusting."

"You didn't seem to think so last night," he said blandly. "And just for the record book, last night had *everything* to do with you and me and *nothing* to do with my bet with George."

"Isn't that why you slept with me?"

"No."

"Then how do you explain that case of Wild Turkey on my front porch?" She made an arrow out of her arm and accusingly pointed toward the front of the house.

"I can't. I don't know how George found out I was here. Maybe he saw me leave the church driving like a madman, followed me out here and drew his own conclusions."

"Or maybe once you'd scored, you sneaked out of bed and came in here to call him."

Ty balefully stared at her for several seconds, then turned his back to take a coffee mug out of the cabinet. Finally, the coffee was ready. Only after he had poured his coffee and taken several scalding sips did he look at her again. "I didn't."

"I don't know that."

"Well, you should. You had your hands on me practically all night." His eyelids lowered sexily. "And what you usually had a hold of I could hardly take out of your clutches without both of us noticing."

Her cheeks filled with color and heat. She lowered her gaze, foundering for something to say. She could feel herself rapidly losing ground and didn't know how to get it back.

"Well, it's over and done with anyway. You won your bet. My week here is up. As soon as my *guest*," she stressed scathingly, "finishes his coffee, I'm leaving for home."

"For New Orleans?"

"Where else?"

"And go back to what?"

"What do you mean by that?" She was immediately on the defensive.

"Back to all those lovers that never existed?"

She had no response to that, so she avoided addressing it at all. "Back to my career."

"A career you could just as easily handle from here." Ty set his empty cup down. "All you'll be going back to is your self-imposed loneliness. You exiled yourself from everything that was familiar and dear to you because you didn't have the guts to stay and face what is so evidently clear."

"That my fiancé chose my bridesmaid over me!"

"No, that you chose the wrong man to begin with. You didn't want to admit to everybody that your judgment had been so far off."

"After what happened, I didn't have any choice but to leave."

"You had plenty of choices!" he shouted. "For one, you could have stayed and married Jenkins. For another, you could have exposed him and Gretchen instead of taking the rap yourself."

"I loved him too much for that," she fired back. She knew it wasn't true; Ty knew it wasn't true. But she wanted to provoke him.

It didn't work. "That's crap, Sunny," he said mildly. "Just like it's crap that your parents left here because of your disgrace."

"What do you know about it?"

"I talked to Fran. She said your dad was offered a fantastic job in Jackson. Their leaving here had nothing to do with you. But you chose to believe it did to justify your own leaving. For the benefit of everybody in Latham Green, you've painted yourself as being an independent career girl with a string of lovers and a devil-take-tomorrow attitude. You started believing in that false image yourself.

"But we both know that woman doesn't exist. That isn't the life you want. When you left here, you weren't running *toward* something. You were running *away*. And if you leave today, that's what you'll be doing again."

Sunny was so angry she was rocking back and forth slightly. "Take your half-baked psychology and go straight to hell, Sheriff Beaumont. I can't wait to get back to New Orleans. I'm leaving as soon as you dress and get out of here."

"Okay," he said with a shrug, "leave. But I'll only come after you."

"What for?"

He moved forward and didn't stop until he was toe to toe with her. "Because I want you. I must be crazy, but I do. I've wanted you since I first saw you eating those damn strawberries. Last night you proved to be the woman I had guessed you were, the woman I've needed and wanted for a long time."

"Well, I hope you enjoyed me because that's the last chance you'll ever get."

He laughed. "Far from it, Sunny. You can run off today, but I'll just chase you down. Remember when I told you that Jenkins was the greater fool for letting you walk through the church door? Well, I'm not Jenkins. I'm gonna stay hot on your saucy little tail until you're in my life, in my house, and in my bed for good."

For a moment Sunny was speechless. "You actually think I would live with you? Here in Latham Green?"

"Husbands and wives usually, not always of course, but usually, live together."

"Husbands and—you think I'm going to marry you?"

He grinned confidently. "Not think. Know."

"You *are* crazy."

"I'm afraid you're right. Most men wouldn't want a firebrand like you around, but I kinda like the excitement. I've been with many women, not a single one of whom has ever gotten me out of bed by flooding the front porch with Wild Turkey," he said, laughing.

"Go ahead, laugh. I think it's hilarious myself that you are under the delusion that I'd ever marry you and live in this hick town."

"This hick town did all right by you. I think it's a great place for kids to grow up."

"Kids?"

"Sure. I think we ought to do our civic duty to keep the Latham Green school district in business, don't you?"

Her expression seethed with mutiny and resentment.

He cuffed her under the chin. "I know you're resistant to the idea right now. You wouldn't recognize what was good and right for you if it came up and bit you. But after you've given it some thought, you'll come around."

He headed for the door. "Oh, and if you do decide to leave today, be quiet while you're packing. As you know, you kept me up most of the night." Scratching his chest absently, he yawned broadly. "I'm going back to bed."

Again Sunny was left staring at an empty doorway.

He was bluffing. Wasn't he?

He hadn't been teasing about the bet with George. He had said he would get her into his bed by the night of the wedding and he had done it.

The idea of marriage was preposterous. Wasn't it?

She loved him. Wouldn't she rather have a life with him in Latham Green than one of loneliness in the city?

No, nothing could change her mind about leaving. Nothing?

This time she would be running from the man she truly loved. From the man who truly—

She poked his bare shoulder. It was infuriating that he had actually gone back to bed and was peacefully sleeping. After the second rough punch to his shoulder, he rolled to his back and blearily looked up at her.

"Are you still here?"

"You never said anything about loving me."

"Is it necessary that I tell you?" He came up on one elbow.

"Well, it would be nice."

He laughed at her testiness. "Sunny, if I hadn't been falling in love, I would have taken you to bed the first day I met you. I would have followed you home from that party and had carnal knowledge of you then and there, gotten you out of my system.

"And—" he said, pointing a warning finger at

her open mouth that dared her to interrupt him, "don't deny that it would have happened. From the first time we looked at each other, it was only a matter of time until we satisfied our attacks of mutual lust. I waited until last night because I was hoping to win your trust, too. I wanted you to know that it wasn't any longer just sex for me."

"Then you meant what you said about liking and admiring the woman I am?"

"Absolutely."

She gnawed on her lower lip. "I don't want more than two children."

He stacked his hands behind his head. "Sounds reasonable, since you're the one who has to have them. You're not too old, are you?"

"Thirty my next birthday," she replied tetchily.

"Thirty, huh? Well, I guess that's okay."

Her temper went into slow simmer. "I won't go dowdy, either. I refuse to change the way I dress to fit the nonfashion trends in this town."

"Good. I like the way you dress." His gaze moved down her body. "And undress."

She resisted his melting look, but it wasn't easy. She felt a familiar weakness in her knees. "I'll have to go into New Orleans frequently."

"I understand."

"I don't intend to give up my work."

"I wouldn't think of asking you to."

"I plan to apply at every bank in Louisiana and Mississippi until I get a loan."

"You won't have to. I have some money set aside."

That shut her up for a moment, then she said, "I won't use your money to start my business."

"Now, Sunny, don't be stubborn. It will be *our* money when we get married." She only stared back at him resolutely. He sighed. "Okay, for once let's compromise. You exhaust all your possibilities, then if none of them pays off, we'll review the situation, keeping my nest egg in mind as a last resort."

She nodded brusquely. "Agreed."

"Anything else?"

"I don't cook very well."

"We won't starve."

"Gardening isn't my thing. I don't like bugs and snakes and dirt and stuff, so don't expect me to enter my homegrown, home-canned green beans in the parish fair."

"Actually I prefer Del Monte."

"I'm neat. I'll expect you to help—"

"Sunny?"

"What?"

"Do you like me?"

She gazed down at his face, thinking that it was the dearest face she'd ever seen, even badly in need of a shave as it was. "Very much."

"Do you love me?"

Emotions welled inside her. She had to swallow hard before saying hoarsely, "Very, *very* much."

He whipped back the covers. "Then shut up and get back in here where you belong."

When she was naked and lying beside him, he gathered her close. "Now that we've got all the technicalities out of the way, now that you know my loving you doesn't pose a threat to your independence, your career, or anything else that makes you you, now that you're *calm*, let me tell you how I feel."

He smoothed back her hair as he whispered huskily, "I love you, Sunny Chandler. I fell in love with you the minute I saw you. Even if I hadn't made the bet with George, I would have wanted you in my bed as soon as possible, and I would have chased you to New Orleans if necessary to get you.

"Whether it's chauvinistic or not, I want to protect you for as long as you live. I'll make certain that everybody knows you are Ty Beaumont's woman, his lady, his wife. Anybody who hurts you will have to deal with me and, as you well know, I can be meaner than hell. You're a pain in the ass and a total delight and I adore you."

Laughing softly, she ran her fingers over his lips. "I could say the same of you." Her eyes were sparkling merrily as she basked in his adoration. "Why didn't you use this romantic approach from the beginning?"

"It never would have worked. I had to let you talk yourself into the idea of loving me."

"Think you're clever, don't you?"

"Immensely," he said without a trace of humility.

She curled her arm around his neck and pulled him down for a deep, lengthy kiss. His hands moved over her lovingly. He touched her breasts and provoked the tender crests until they beaded against his stroking fingers. Lowering his head, he kissed them in turn and laved them with his tongue.

They caressed, perfectly attuned to each other's desire. Soon, their breathing was choppy and swift.

"Ty," she sighed, "don't touch me there."

"You don't like it?"

"Yes, yes, but if you don't stop, it'll be all over for me before you've even started."

"Want to make a bet on that, Sunny Chandler?"

THE EDITOR'S CORNER

I'm really impressed with the talent so many of you display for writing heart-wrenching letters! I get a lot of them about how long you have to wait for good reading between groups of LOVESWEPTs. For all of you who feel that way—and especially those of you who've written to me—I have a special FLASH bulletin. On sale right now is a fabulous novel that I believe you will want to read immediately. It's from Bantam (of course!) and is titled **WILD MIDNIGHT**. It's written by a wonderfully talented and versatile author named Maggie Davis. For a long time I've had a hunch that many women would enjoy as much as I a tale combining a number of elements: fiery sensuality, thoroughly up-to-date gothic elements in a completely believable context, and—most of all—primary characters one can really care about and root for. Trouble was, no one was writing such a book. Then along came Maggie Davis. **WILD MIDNIGHT** has thrills and chills, twists and turns galore, and a wonderfully torrid and touching romance between two unforgettable lovers. Grab a copy while you can!

As always, we're delighted to bring you a brand-new talent: Susan Richardson. Susan's first published novel is **FIDDLIN' FOOL**, LOVESWEPT #186. When an utterly charming Scottish rogue and accomplished fiddler, Jamie McLeod, performs in Sarah Hughes's hometown, he manages to turn her world upside down! His music is as wild, free, and utterly mesmerizing as the man himself. Sarah is captivated—but still part of her holds back, not believing the magic between her and Jamie could ever last. You'll be as enchanted as Sarah when Jamie sets out to woo her with thrilling music and sweet seduction.

A long time ago I read that Louisa May Alcott said that when she wrote she was "swept into a vortex" from which there was no escape (not even for sleeping or eating) until her tale was put on paper. Now, Iris

(continued)

Johansen tells me she doesn't write in the way that Ms. Alcott did, but the effect for the reader certainly is one of being "swept into a vortex." And nowhere is that storytelling power of Iris's more evident than in LOVESWEPT #187, **LAST BRIDGE HOME**. Elizabeth Ramsey is soon to give birth to the child of her late husband Mark, who was tragically killed in an auto accident during Elizabeth's first weeks of pregnancy. Then Jon Sandell, a stranger claiming to be Mark's best friend, moves into Elizabeth's life, ostensibly to protect her. But soon she realizes that her heart, her soul, belong to Jon and that the jeopardy he has told her she's in is very real indeed. This marvelous, complex love story—full of surprises—is one that I bet you'll never forget.

Again, it is a real delight for us to be able to introduce a new writer. Becky Lee Weyrich publishes her first contemporary romance novel with us. (You may have seen some of Becky's exciting long historical novels on bookracks in the last couple of years.) Becky debuts in **DETOUR TO EUPHORIA,** LOVESWEPT #188, a dilly of a book that's set in a small town in Georgia. From Sibyl Blanchard's arrest by the local sheriff to her near cardiac arrest over the charms of local lawyer Nick Fremont, who comes to bail her out, **DETOUR TO EUPHORIA** is a straight road into delightful romance. Nick brings Sibyl to his family's plantation house, and she feels as though she's stepped into a dream . . . until the time for her appearance in court draws near, and with it the end of her detour into Nick's arms. We predict you're going to grow very fond of each and every one of the wildly, wonderfully Southern (and infinitely believable) characters in this love story . . . and that you'll never forget a little Georgia town named Euphoria.

Be prepared to chuckle . . . and cheer . . . and be downright enchanted by Kay Hooper's **IN SERENA'S WEB,** LOVESWEPT #189! This is "vintage" Kay telling the story of Serena Jameson, who has the look of

(continued)

an angel, the sexiness of a true temptress, and the devilish determination of Satan himself. Why, Serena can be nothing short of ruthless when she makes up her mind to get something and there's a wee obstacle or two in the way! Poor Brian Ashford! You have to feel just a little bit sorry for the handsome industrialist as he gets drawn into our heroine's web. He even thinks *he's* protecting *her*—from playboy Joshua Long, among others. Then Serena gets a double-whammy she richly deserves, and you'll be right on the edge of your chair as danger and desire tangle the lives of these delightful people. Be sure to pay strict attention to that rakish Joshua, because Kay isn't through with him, not by a long shot! Am I teasing you mercilessly? Just in case I am, I'll give you a sneak preview: Stay tuned for **RAVEN ON THE WING,** LOVESWEPT #193, by Kay, coming next month.

Warm wishes,

Sincerely,

Carolyn Nichols

Carolyn Nichols
   Editor
LOVESWEPT
Bantam Books, Inc.
666 Fifth Avenue
New York, NY 10103

*Heirs to a great dynasty, the Delaney
brothers were united by blood, united by
devotion to their rugged land . . . and
known far and wide as*

THE SHAMROCK
TRINITY

Bantam's bestselling LOVESWEPT romance line built its reputation on quality and innovation. Now, a remarkable and unique event in romance publishing comes from the same source: THE SHAMROCK TRINITY, three daringly original novels written by three of the most successful women's romance writers today. Kay Hooper, Iris Johansen, and Fayrene Preston have created a trio of books that are dynamite love stories bursting with strong, fascinating male and female characters, deeply sensual love scenes, the humor for which LOVESWEPT is famous, and a deliciously fresh approach to romance writing.

*THE SHAMROCK TRINITY—Burke, York, and
Rafe: Powerful men . . . rakes and charmers . . .
they needed only love to make their lives complete.*

☐ *RAFE, THE MAVERICK by Kay Hooper*

Rafe Delaney was a heartbreaker whose ebony eyes held laughing devils and whose lilting voice could charm any lady—or any horse—until a stallion named Diablo left him in the dust. It took Maggie O'Riley to work her magic on the impossible horse . . . and on his bold owner. Maggie's grace and strength made Rafe yearn to share the raw beauty of his land with her, to teach her the exquisite pleasure of yielding to the heat inside her. Maggie was stirred by Rafe's passion, but would his reputation and her ambition keep their kindred spirits apart?   (21786 • $2.50)

 # LOVESWEPT

X

☐ *YORK, THE RENEGADE by Iris Johansen*

Some men were made to fight dragons, Sierra Smith thought when she first met York Delaney. The rebel brother had roamed the world for years before calling the rough mining town of Hell's Bluff home. Now, the spirited young woman who'd penetrated this renegade's paradise had awakened a savage and tender possessiveness in York: something he never expected to find in himself. Sierra had known loneliness and isolation too—enough to realize that York's restlessness had only to do with finding a place to belong. Could she convince him that love was such a place, that the refuge he'd always sought was in her arms?

(21787 • $2.50)

☐ *BURKE, THE KINGPIN by Fayrene Preston*

Cara Winston appeared as a fantasy, racing on horseback to catch the day's last light—her silver hair glistening, her dress the color of the Arizona sunset . . . and Burke Delaney wanted her. She was on his horse, on his land: she would have to belong to him too. But Cara was quicksilver, impossible to hold, a wild creature whose scent was midnight flowers and sweet grass. Burke had always taken what he wanted, by willing it or fighting for it; Cara cherished her freedom and refused to believe his love would last. Could he make her see he'd captured her to have and hold forever?

(21788 • $2.50)